Payback

PAUL LANGAN

Originally published as *The Gun*

Series Editor: Paul Langan

SCHOLASTIC INC.

New York Toronto London Auckland Sydney
Mexico City New Delhi Hong Kong Buenos Aires

Originally published as *The Gun*.
No part of this publication may be reproduced,
stored in a retrieval system, or transmitted in any form
or by any means, electronic, mechanical, photocopying,
recording, or otherwise, without written permission of the publisher.
For information regarding permission, write to Townsend Press, Inc.,
1038 Industrial Drive, West Berlin, NJ 08091.
Visit Townsend Press on the Web at
www.townsendpress.com.

ISBN-13: 978-0-439-90487-2
ISBN-10: 0-439-90487-0

12 11 10 9 8 7 6 5   8 9 10 11 12/0

Printed in the U.S.A.   01

First Scholastic printing, June 2007

Chapter 1

Man, I hate this place, Tyray Hobbs thought as he walked slowly towards Bluford High School. The motion from each step sent a dull jab of pain into his left wrist, making him wince slightly.

Just outside Bluford's thick steel front doors, Tyray adjusted his jacket, careful to conceal the bone-colored cast which now encased his left hand. The pain and cast were constant reminders of the humiliation he suffered four days ago.

Until then, Tyray had been the most notorious bully in Bluford's freshman class. Six feet tall and muscular, he could clear a path in a crowd just by showing up. In middle school, Tyray had learned to use his size to intimidate people he didn't like. Sometimes, he impressed his friends by forcing smaller boys to give him money or do his homework. Other times, he threatened kids for fun. At Bluford, Tyray's reputation continued to grow. And then Darrell Mercer came along.

The first time they met, Tyray thought Darrell was the perfect target—a scrawny, weak kid who transferred to Bluford in the middle of the school year. Having just moved from Philadelphia days earlier, Darrell didn't know a soul in California, and he was scared. A punching bag with legs, Tyray thought. He had recognized the fear in Darrell's eyes from day one. After a bit of pressure, Darrell was giving Tyray his lunch money each week in hopes of being left alone. It was some of the easiest money Tyray had ever made. But four days ago, everything changed. The incident replayed in his mind like a scene from an old movie.

It happened at lunchtime in the crowded school cafeteria. Tyray was hassling Darrell for skipping his weekly payment. To embarrass him, Tyray tipped Darrell's lunch tray, spilling food all over the smaller boy's clothes. The trick worked. Kids throughout the cafeteria howled at Darrell's mess.

Then Darrell did something he had never done before. He stood up to Tyray in front of everyone.

"Tyray, you ain't nothing but a bully," Darrell called out. "No one in this school likes you. They are just afraid of you. But you know what? I ain't afraid of you no more. You don't scare me." He then demanded that Tyray apologize and clean up the mess.

Tyray was shocked at the smaller boy's bold words. It was true that Darrell had started acting more confident, especially since he befriended Mr. Mitchell, their nosy English teacher, and joined the Bluford wrestling team. But Darrell was still a coward. Tyray never expected him to stand up for himself.

Careful not to show his surprise, Tyray stepped over to beat Darrell into a pulp right there in front of everyone. But Darrell was fast. The next thing Tyray knew, Darrell had swept underneath him, lifted him up, and sent him crashing onto the hard floor of the cafeteria.

Tyray tried to cushion the fall with his left arm, but the impact cracked his wrist bone with a loud wet snap. He could not believe the amount of pain he felt. A nonstop knifing ache mingled with the sensation that the inside of his wrist was on fire.

Worse than the pain was seeing that

kids who once feared him were laughing. Some even cheered.

After the fight, Tyray was taken straight to the nurse's office. He was still fuming in the wake of his defeat, and his wrist was swelling by the minute. The nurse's reaction to his injury did not comfort him any.

"We've got to get you to a hospital," she said. "Your wrist doesn't look good at all, Mr. Hobbs. We'll have to call one of your parents to meet you there."

Great, Tyray thought to himself. *Just great.*

It was Mom who met Tyray and the school nurse at the Emergency Room of City General Hospital. For Tyray, sitting in the waiting room in pain for two hours was nothing compared to enduring his mother's coddling the entire time.

Once the nurse left, Mom looked at Tyray with a pitiful face. At one point, she even had tears in her eyes. "Mom, I'm fine," he insisted. Looking at her made him feel even worse about what happened. He did not want her there, but the school required a parent or guardian to be at the hospital with him. Tyray knew Mom was the only person he could turn to. Calling Dad never even crossed his mind.

"Honey, I hate to see you in pain," Mom said, her voice breaking. "And I hate to see you in trouble. We have an appointment to see the principal first thing tomorrow morning. You might get suspended—or even worse."

Tyray tried to shrug off the whole thing. "So what," he said. "I don't care about school. That principal's wacked anyway."

"Well, I care," Mom responded. "And so should you. I didn't want to believe the things that woman told me over the phone. I couldn't believe my ears. All those tales about you bullying kids and beating up on people. Tyray, it just breaks my heart. And your father won't be pleased by this at all."

Tyray knew Mom was right. His father would definitely not be pleased, but Tyray could not worry about that yet. He was still in a great deal of pain. And every time he thought about the fight in the cafeteria, he trembled with rage. Even as the doctor slowly wrapped his wrist, he was seething in silence.

He was not done with Darrell Mercer.

The next morning before his first class, Tyray and his mother met with Ms. Spencer, the school principal, who was sitting stern-faced at her desk. Tyray knew by the tightness in her jaw that he was in big trouble. He just did not know how severe the punishment would be. Would he be suspended? Expelled?

"Good morning, Mrs. Hobbs, Tyray," Ms. Spencer said, an icy edge to her voice. She took a sip of coffee from a mug and turned to him. "I've heard Darrell's side of this story. What do you have to say for yourself?"

"Wasn't my fault," Tyray mumbled. "Mercer started with me."

"I suggest you tell me the truth, Mr. Hobbs," Ms. Spencer said, her voice filled with contempt. "We know how you have been bullying and intimidating other students. These are serious accusations. I suggest you tell me everything you know."

As his mother listened, her eyes filled with tears. "Please, Tyray," she whispered. "Just tell the truth."

"I ain't done nothin' wrong. All you hearin' is lies," Tyray began, but the anger in Ms. Spencer's face stopped him right there.

"Mr. Hobbs, you are very close to being expelled from this high school. Do you understand what I am saying?" Ms. Spencer growled.

Tyray imagined what his father's reaction would be if he got expelled. Tyray was big, but his father was twice his size. In his high school days, Gil Hobbs was an offensive lineman on the football team, standing a solid six foot four inches and weighing almost three hundred pounds. Tyray knew his father would be furious if he got expelled. He shuddered as he thought of his father's response to such news.

"Okay, okay," Tyray said to the principal.

"Not 'okay, okay,'" Ms. Spencer snapped. "That won't cut it around here. It's 'I understand, Ms. Spencer.'"

Tyray was not used to being put in his place, not even by teachers. He felt a burning rage for the skinny woman glaring at him behind wire rim glasses. But she had the power now. So Tyray swallowed hard and mumbled, "I understand, Ms. Spencer."

"Good," the principal said crisply. "Now then, you will be suspended for three days for fighting and for bullying other students. The suspension begins at once. And if there is ever any more bullying, Mr. Hobbs, I'll see to it that you are out of this school permanently." ·

"Don't worry, Ms. Spencer," Tyray's mother said, wiping her eyes. "I know Tyray's sorry, and I'm sure he'll behave from now on."

"I hope so," Ms. Spencer added. "For *his* sake."

Tyray shrugged his shoulders but said nothing. Ms. Spencer's threats were nothing compared to what was waiting for him at home when his father found out about the suspension.

"You little punk!" Dad screamed later that night. "Where you get off fightin' and messin' around in school and gettin' your hand busted?"

"Gil," Mom said in her soft voice, "he's in a lot of pain—"

"Woman, don't give me that!" Dad yelled, causing Mom to cower. "You been coddlin' this boy all his life, and that's why we got this kind of trouble with him now. I'm glad he's in pain, understand? Now leave us alone."

Mom hurried out of the room, lines of worry creasing her forehead. Tyray knew she was just as afraid of Dad as he was. He could count on his mother to protect him only so much.

Dad grabbed hold of Tyray's shirt collar, lifting him so that their faces were only inches apart. "What you got to say for yourself, boy?" he growled.

Tyray shrugged, and his father flicked his finger into his face, bruising his lip. Tyray winced in pain. Dad had done this to him many times before. It was the same thing Tyray had done to Darrell when they first met.

"How come you been beatin' up on other kids and gettin' the whole school on your case?" As he spoke, Dad shook Tyray violently and shoved him into a corner of the kitchen, sending pots clattering to the floor. "You cost me money, boy. I got to pay to get your hand fixed. Cash money that coulda gone for food, rent, or clothes, y'see?"

With his last words, Dad opened his hand and slapped Tyray across the mouth. The force of the blow split Tyray's lip. A thread of blood sliding down his chin, he cringed, waiting for another strike.

"I'm sorry," Tyray gasped, covering his face with his hands.

"Sorry? Sorry is words, cheap words. They don't mean nothing. You'd be sorry if we didn't get your wrist fixed. That's what you deserve. I feel like smashin' that cast and bustin' your wrist all over again. Then you'd be real sorry," Dad said.

"Gil, please," Mom pleaded from the hallway, fear heavy in her voice. "Isn't that enough?"

"What?!" Dad yelled at her. "Woman, didn't I tell you to stay out of this? We already lost one son, and I ain't about to lose another."

Mom vanished down the hall, and his father gave Tyray a final, violent shake of his shoulders. "You get in any trouble during the next three days, I swear I'll bust your other hand." He shoved Tyray away and stormed out of the kitchen.

Tyray jumped to his feet and rushed to the bedroom he used to share with Warren, his older brother. Warren had been gone now for over a year. He was serving a three-year sentence for armed robbery.

Tyray wished he never had to face Dad again. He was always unsure how he felt about his father. At times, he admired the way Dad was boss wherever he went. Even at work, he ruled with an iron fist. A foreman for a construction company, he towered over his entire crew. Everyone knew not to get on Gil Hobbs's bad side. But more than respecting his father, Tyray feared him. He had learned long ago that the safest way to deal with Dad was to stay out of his way. It had worked pretty well until Darrell Mercer came along.

Now, Tyray was returning to Bluford for the first time since Ms. Spencer suspended him three days ago. As he got closer to school, he felt a growing sense of dread. The teachers and the principal would be watching his every move. So would the students. Some might even hassle him about losing the fight with Darrell. Hundreds of students had watched Tyray writhing on the floor with his broken wrist. Three days was not enough time for them to forget what they saw.

Walking down the main corridor of the school, Tyray sensed many eyes watching him. He noticed several students glance in his direction and then quickly look away. Their faces were like

11

billboards with one message. *Yeah, we've been talking about you since you went down*, they seemed to say.

As he approached his locker, Tyray was glad to see Rodney Banks. Rodney and Tyray had become friends in middle school. They discovered then that ganging up on smaller kids was easy and profitable. Rodney loved sharing in all the cash they extorted from scared students. He often used his cut of the money to buy the latest athletic gear, especially basketball sneakers.

"Hey, Rod," Tyray called out as he neared his friend. Rodney quickly turned away and darted into a crowd of students. Tyray watched bitterly as Rodney disappeared down the hallway. He remembered all the times the two of them went to the mall to buy jackets with team logos. Now Rodney was turning like the dog who bit the hand that fed him. "Forget you, then," Tyray mumbled.

Several students stared at Tyray as he continued down the long corridor to his first class. At one point, he thought he heard a girl snicker. Then, he spotted someone pointing to his cast.

"Whatcha lookin' at?" Tyray yelled when he reached the end of the hall. A heavy silence spread through the corridor. Tyray turned the corner and continued walking. "Just wait," he muttered. "Gonna be payback time for y'all. Just you wait."

Then he spotted Darrell Mercer walking with Amberlynn Bailey.

Instantly Tyray's pulse started to pound. Watching Darrell talk to Amberlynn, Tyray was filled with hatred. He would hide his feelings for now, but soon Darrell's time would come. Nothing would feel better than wiping that big smile off Darrell's face.

"I'm sorry about your hand," a girl said from behind Tyray as he walked towards English class.

Tyray turned to see Lark Collins, a freshman he hardly knew. She was cute, in a wholesome way, but his tastes ran to more striking girls. There were a lot of girls eager to mess with a bad boy, especially one as big as Tyray. Even though he was not that handsome, girls seemed drawn to him because of his reputation. But now, he wondered if all that would change too. And he wondered why a girl like Lark was suddenly being nice to him.

"Yeah, I bet you're sorry," Tyray said, moving his broken wrist out of her sight.

"I *am*," Lark insisted, her eyes widening.

"You for real?" Tyray asked gruffly.

"Yeah, I'm just sorry you broke your wrist, that's all."

"You see it happen?"

"No, I was in the library that day," Lark responded.

"But, you heard about it?" Tyray asked, tensing up.

"Sure. Everyone's been talking about it," Lark answered. Tyray cringed slightly, and Lark seemed to understand what he was feeling. "Don't worry. I try to stay out of everyone's gossip. Half of it usually isn't true anyway. I just feel bad for you, that's all."

Tyray looked closely at Lark. She was not the prettiest girl at Bluford, not by a mile. She was slightly overweight, and her glasses and frumpy clothes made her look a bit like an old lady. Yet she seemed sincere.

Before the fight in the cafeteria, Tyray would not even have spoken to someone like Lark. But now that he was alone at Bluford, he was in no position to chase people away. Besides, maybe he could use her. Lark would not be as stubborn or demanding as the girls who used to

14

flirt with him. A few harsh words, and she would skitter off in tears and never talk to him again. Tyray read this in her face the same way he read the fear in Darrell's eyes months ago. Lark was someone he could manipulate.

"You wanna eat lunch with me today?" Tyray asked.

Lark paused a moment and then answered, "Sure. That would be nice."

"Okay. Meet me in the cafeteria at lunchtime," Tyray said, before heading off to English.

Tyray used to swagger into classes, pausing to send menacing glares into the faces of kids he was trying to scare. It had been so exciting for Tyray to see them hunkering in their seats and wishing they were invisible. But now, he didn't glare at anybody.

Sitting down at his desk, Tyray opened his English book to a story he had not read and did not care about. He glanced at the meaningless words and sentences on the pages and noticed Harold Davis watching him. Harold was Darrell Mercer's closest friend. Until a few days ago, he was too scared to even look at Tyray. *Things sure have turned around,* Tyray thought, certain Harold was silently laughing at him.

"*Look at the big bully with the broken wrist. He cried just like a baby,*" Tyray imagined Harold saying.

Just you wait, Tyray thought over and over. *Just you wait.* His day of revenge would come, and no one would ever forget it. Especially not Darrell Mercer.

Chapter 2

Tyray and Lark sat together at an unoccupied table in the cafeteria. Being back in that room made Tyray uneasy. As he ate his lunch, he tried to avoid looking at the spot where Darrell had thrown him to the floor.

"The only time I ever had to go to the hospital was when I was a little girl. I fell down my grandma's steps and busted my lip open," Lark said, interrupting Tyray's thoughts. She was staring at a small straw which she twisted around her fingers as she spoke. "The doctor stitched it up. I guess you can't notice it now unless you really look for the little scar."

Tyray had not noticed anything unusual until Lark mentioned it. "Oh yeah, I see where they fixed it," he said, leaning in closer to examine her face. A tiny scar ran along the top of her upper lip.

Lark suddenly got quiet. Tyray thought she might have been waiting for him to say something nice to her. But that was not Tyray's style. No one ever said nice things to him, and he was not about to treat her any differently. Being nice to people was weak. Not being nice gave you an edge. Tyray's father said that a lot, and Tyray believed it. Dad said he never praised the men in his crew because they would think he was soft and then try to take advantage of him.

"Gotta keep 'em guessin'," Dad once said. *"I like keepin' 'em afraid their work isn't up to snuff and maybe they gonna get laid off. Make 'em afraid to take time off when they got a little bellyache or somethin'. It's the way things gotta be done, boy. That's the way a man handles his business."*

Lark reached up and touched the small scar. "Mom's always telling me it doesn't show. But I guess that's a mom for you, huh?" she said, with a faint sigh.

"Yeah, they think lyin' to you is better than hearing you whine about somethin'," Tyray answered between bites of his hot dog. He hated the cafeteria food. He often joked that it tasted like erasers and chalk. On days when his and Rodney's pockets were full with other kids' money, they often headed for a fast food joint right after school to get "real" food. Little chance of that now.

Just then, Tyray noticed Darrell and Amberlynn laughing and talking at a nearby table. Amberlynn immediately caught him watching her and turned away.

Tyray knew she hated him. Even though she used to flirt with him and he once told her he liked her, the two were now enemies. He shot her a mocking smile before turning his attentions back to Lark.

"Know what, baby?" Tyray said smoothly.

Lark blinked. "What?"

"You got beautiful eyes," Tyray said.

"*Me*?" Lark asked, excitement in her voice.

"They're beautiful, and they cast a magic spell," he added. He had learned there were times to be sweet too, especially to get what you wanted. For years, he watched Dad turn on the charm whenever Mom cashed her paycheck. She would be planning to go down to the store and get herself a new dress, but

Dad would sweet-talk her out of half her money. He would throw her a little compliment, like you would throw a dog a bone, and she would hand over the cash.

"Nobody's ever said anything about my eyes before," Lark said softly, turning her head away.

"Well, it's true," Tyray replied. "I ain't never seen no girl with eyes like those. You could be a model in a magazine."

"Are you kidding me?" Lark asked.

"I'm serious, girl."

A big smile spread over Lark's lips, making the tiny scar vanish entirely. *She does have a pretty smile*, he admitted to himself.

Then, over Lark's shoulder, Tyray saw Amberlynn walking over to their table. He smirked at her as she approached, but she acted as if she didn't see him. "Lark, why don't you come eat lunch with us next time?"

"Okay," Lark said awkwardly. "Tyray asked me to eat lunch with him today, and we've been having a nice time. Maybe one day we can all—"

"We'll talk in science class," Amberlynn cut in, her eyes narrowing.

Tyray was about to send Amberlynn running with a harsh insult. But he remembered Ms. Spencer's warning and did not want to give her any excuse to punish him. One bad incident and he would be out of Bluford for good.

Then his father would deal with him. Tyray did not want to face his wrath again. He was never quite sure how far his father would go. When he was a boy, Tyray had overheard his brother Warren tell friends stories about how Dad had beaten up men who crossed him, leaving them draped in garbage cans in dark alleys. As he got older, Tyray suspected some of the stories were lies meant to impress neighborhood kids, but some of them were probably true.

After Amberlynn left, Lark said, "I was looking in an old yearbook from Lincoln High School, and I saw pictures of your father. My Dad went to Lincoln back in the day too, but he wasn't a football hero. Your Dad was practically on every page of the yearbook. I bet you're proud of him."

"Yeah," Tyray said bitterly. He had seen the pictures too. Dad in his football uniform. Dad making a block. Dad running interference. Dad as most valuable player. When Tyray was younger, he hoped to be a big football star too, just like Dad. That would have been a way to be somebody despite his lousy grades. But Tyray lacked his father's talent. He constantly fumbled the ball, and his low grades made it a constant struggle just to be eligible for sports.

"Did your father ever play football in college?" Lark asked.

"He got a college football scholarship," Tyray said, "but when he got there, some teachers didn't like him. He lost the scholarship . . . ruined his chances."

"That's so sad," Lark said.

Tyray rolled his eyes at his own words. He knew he was just repeating his father's old lie. He had heard the story many times before about how the college teachers had it in for Dad because he was black. That they resented a smart black athlete and deliberately sabotaged his future just because of his skin color. Tyray heard repeatedly about how Gil Hobbs would have eventually been drafted by the Broncos or the Cowboys and ended up rich and famous. But out of pure racism, those college teachers ruined his plans.

Tyray knew such things happened, but not to his father. The truth was Gil Hobbs just could not get good grades.

Not any more than Tyray. That was the truth, and the truth hurt. Tyray understood that. Dad had made up the lie to hide the fact that he was a poor student.

When he was younger, Tyray was also ashamed that he could not get good grades. In middle school, he would often break into a cold sweat before tests, and he just could not seem to focus on books or what his teachers said. To hide his embarrassment, he practiced the one thing he was good at—bullying. Such behavior stopped other kids from picking on him. By eighth grade, Tyray was so big and tough that he got his way without being school smart. And it worked, until now.

"I bet your Dad is really mad about what happened," Lark said. "Those athletes make such good money."

"Yeah," Tyray said. "He's mad all right. Real mad. He won't even watch football on TV. Me and my brother used to sneak over to a neighbor's house to watch it." Tyray stopped himself. He could not believe he was sharing a personal story with Lark. Even girls he liked did not get him to say so much about himself. He had to remember to keep his guard up.

After lunch, Tyray went to Mr. Fitch's history class. Mr. Fitch was a short, balding man who always wore gray suits and hardly ever smiled. The tone of his voice made Tyray sleepy. He was nothing like Mr. Mitchell, who wore shirts with cartoon characters on them and told funny stories. Mr. Fitch even bored the students who liked history.

When Tyray sat down in the back row, Kendra Wilson, a girl who used to like him, whispered something to her friend. Tyray could not hear what they were saying, but he knew they were talking about him. Then she spoke loudly enough for the back half of the class to hear. "Hey, he don't look so big anymore, does he? Looks like he shrunk!"

The girls laughed hysterically. Even Harold Davis smiled. Tyray clenched his hands into fists, struggling not to throw his chair across the room at everyone who laughed at him.

Tyray wanted his old world back. He wanted things to be as they were before Darrell came to Bluford.

At the end of the day, Tyray bolted from Bluford, which felt more like a prison than a high school. Halfway home, he stopped in front of a fast-food restaurant, eager to grab a burger and forget the day's humiliation. But when he reached into his pocket, he found only enough change for a soda. Weeks ago, he had money to buy anything he wanted, but not anymore.

"Looks like his wrist ain't the only thing that's broke," said a voice behind him, followed by a chorus of laughter. Tyray turned to see a group of Bluford students walking by on their way into the restaurant.

"You keep talkin', and your face is gonna be broke too," Tyray shot back as the kids passed. One girl snickered as she opened the door and went inside. Though no one else said anything, the damage was done. Tyray's face burned in anger. Frustrated, he cursed loudly and kicked the restaurant door, sending a knife of pain into his foot.

"Hey, boy, you best get outta here before I call the police," said a middle-aged employee who suddenly came out of the restaurant.

"Yeah, whatever," Tyray growled, spitting on the ground defiantly. Frustrated, he turned to head home when he noticed a tall, skinny man standing on the corner ahead of him. The man was watching him closely. At first, Tyray ignored the man, who remained statue-like, but then he recognized the face.

The man's name was Bones, and he was practically a legend in the neighborhood. Years ago, Warren had hung out with him for a while, even bringing him to the house once. Bones was a guy everyone feared, someone people sought when they needed something illegal. Though he hadn't seen Bones much since Warren went to jail, Tyray had heard plenty. Countless rumors pointed to Bones as the suspect in many area crimes. Others said Bones had actually committed a number of gang-related hits.

Whatever the story, Tyray was in awe of the man. Nobody messed with Bones.

"What's up, little brother?" Bones asked, his voice crackling like dry leaves. "How'd you hurt that hand?"

"What's up, Bones," Tyray answered nervously, covering his fractured wrist. "I got problems in school. People messin' with me."

Bones lowered his head thoughtfully. "Hard to get respect in this world sometimes," he said.

"I used to get lots of respect," Tyray replied, studying Bones's face, which seemed gaunt and prematurely aged. "Nobody dissed me. But this little punk snuck up on me and caught me off point. Now everybody's dissin' me bad."

Without a word, Bones nodded towards an alley and started walking. Tyray was puzzled for an instant, but he quickly followed. As they turned into the alley, Bones reached into his coat with a swift, smooth motion. He had the quickest hands Tyray had ever seen—like a magician doing a sleight-of-hand trick. In a split second, a gray metal object appeared between his fingers. Tyray's jaw dropped as he realized Bones was holding a small gun. Its shiny steel barrel glimmered in the afternoon sun.

"Here's respect, boy," Bones said, holding out the gun.

Tyray felt his heart flutter as if someone had jolted him with a spike of electricity. He reached out instinctively to touch the gun, but Bones withdrew it with catlike speed. He smiled at Tyray for the first time. Two of his front teeth were gold capped. Others, long and discolored, looked like fangs.

"You sellin' it?" Tyray asked eagerly.

"Maybe," Bones said.

Tyray felt as if the world had suddenly shifted. Everything seemed different somehow. *A gun*, he thought, as a feeling of excitement and relief spread through his veins. *A gun is the answer.* It was a way of turning back the clock. With a gun, no one at Bluford would laugh at him. No one would dare disrespect him again. Instead, they would cower in his presence.

"I want that gun, man," Tyray said.

Bones chuckled, a sickening rattling sound coming from his chest. "We'll see," he nodded. "We'll see how bad you want it."

"What do you mean?" Tyray demanded. For an instant, he forgot his fear of Bones. "Why'd you show me the gun if you ain't gonna sell it?"

"You think about it some more, little brother. Let it stew for a while. I owe it to Warren to make you think on this one. He made his choice, and he's livin' with it. Before you go down the same path, you best do some thinkin'."

"I don't need to think about nothin'. I need the gun now," Tyray insisted, his voice rising in desperation. After what happened in the cafeteria, Tyray saw no other way to get his reputation back.

And he could not tolerate more days like the one he just had. He had no more patience, not even with Bones. "How long do I have to wait?"

Bones took a raspy breath and stared at Tyray, his eyes cold and serious. "This time next week, meet me in the restaurant. Bring fifty dollars with you."

"Next week!" Tyray cried. "That's too long!"

"The wait will do you good, little man," Bones said. "You're a baby yet. A little baby. That's what I see. This time next week, we'll see if you've done some growing up."

As Bones strutted away, Tyray heard him coughing with a violent, chest-shaking rattle.

Tyray turned slowly and continued his walk home, his heart racing at the thought of the gun.

Chapter 3

Tyray was glad to arrive home before his father. Dad usually came home in a bad mood. Mom would rush around making dinner, trying to keep the peace and stay out of his way. But even she could not avoid catching blasts of his foul temper.

"This house is filthy! Can't you do anything right?" he would often complain.

"Gil, I just cleaned it yesterday. The only mess I see is from your work boots," Mom would reply softly.

"You want to start an argument tonight, don't you?" Dad would shout, slamming doors and stomping around the house like a drunken elephant. Then he would settle down in his chair in front of the TV, his dinner on a metal tray on his lap. Within a few minutes after he finished eating, he would begin snoring in his chair, and peace would return to the house.

During such times, Tyray would look at his father and remember what he once said. *"I might not be the smartest man in the world. And I ain't the best lookin' neither. But you better believe that folks are gonna respect me 'cause they know I ain't scared of nothin'. I don't care who I'm talking to. I just look 'em in their eyes, and they're afraid 'cause they know I can hurt 'em. All the education in the world still ain't too much for the fear I put in folks. That's all I need."*

Tyray had accepted that philosophy for himself long ago. Like his father, he knew he wasn't as smart as other kids, at least not at school. His brother Warren had always been a stronger student than Tyray. Warren was better-looking, too. He looked more like Mom, tall and slender with nice, well-shaped features. Tyray, on the other hand, had inherited his appearance from his father. As a boy, he hated his stocky body, thick neck, and square jaw, features which made him stand out from his peers.

"I'm ugly," Tyray wailed when he was eight, after a group of older kids chased him home, taunting him.

"Moose," they had called him over and over again. *"That boy look like a big old ugly moose."*

"Don't take nothin' from them, Tyray. And never let them see you cry," Warren had said, chasing the boys away. *"Anytime anyone give you trouble, you send 'em to me. That's what brothers are for, you got that?"*

Tyray wished his brother was home and able to help him. But Tyray knew he had to handle this problem alone. And the only way he could see getting his respect back was by owning a gun. That alone would rescue him from the dark hole into which he had fallen.

Saturday finally came, and Tyray decided to try to get a gun before his meeting with Bones. He just could not wait a whole week, not with daily humiliations at Bluford.

Tyray knew he could buy almost anything in the neighborhood after dark. Just last year, Londell James got a gun and used it to shoot Roylin Bailey, Amberlynn's older brother. Even though Roylin was only grazed, Londell became one of the most feared kids on the street. Just mentioning his name made many kids nervous. Tyray hoped one day that his own name would have the same effect on people. No matter what, he just had to get that gun.

Near the corner of Cypress Street, Tyray saw two guys on bikes and a couple of others shooting baskets at a hoop bolted to the side of an abandoned building. Tyray recognized them immediately. Cedric Hodden and Shamar Briggs were the two kids jumping curbs on bikes. They were both in his freshman class. Eddie Bryson and Len Staley, two Bluford dropouts, were the ones shooting baskets. Tyray was certain one of them could help him find a gun. Taking a deep breath, he edged towards the makeshift basketball court.

"Whassup guys, how y'all doin'?" Tyray asked. He knew Eddie and Len from middle school. In the seventh grade, he got money from Len by shoving and smacking him around a bit. Len seemed pretty scared at the time, but that was years ago. Len had probably forgotten about it by now, Tyray thought.

"I remember you," Len said, stepping back when Tyray approached. "You the dude that us'ta steal my lunch money. Whatcha want?"

"He did that?" Eddie asked, before Tyray could answer.

"Yeah," Len replied. "Roughed me up a few times, even when I didn't have anything to give him."

"Man, that was just kid stuff," Tyray said, extending his hand to Len. "We way past that now."

"Wasn't kid stuff when I went hungry at lunchtime 'cause you stole my money," Len snapped.

Tyray noticed both boys were staring at the cast on his broken wrist. His heartbeat quickened slightly, and sweat began to form on his brow.

Just then, Cedric and Shamar rode over on their bikes. Shamar began laughing when he spotted Tyray. "Hey Hobbs, you looked so funny layin' on the floor in the cafeteria after Mercer clocked you."

"He got beat up at school?" Len asked Cedric excitedly. "Did you see it happen?"

Tyray felt his stomach twisting into knots. He could see what was happening, but there was no way to stop it.

"Yeah, I was right there," Cedric said, getting off his bike. "This little dude, Darrell Mercer, smallest kid in our class, pounded him, and that's how he got his wrist busted. You shoulda seen him. He was rolling on the floor cryin' like a baby. 'It's broke, it's broke!'" Cedric's last words were a screeching imitation of a child's voice.

"Didn't happen like that," Tyray protested.

"Yeah, it did," Shamar said, laughing. "You got beat down. Mercer took you down proper."

Raucous laughter erupted from all four boys. The sound was sharp and piercing, stabbing at Tyray like bee stings.

"You better watch your mouth," he snarled. "I can whip all y'all. Ain't no doubt about that. I can do it, bad wrist and all. So don't be playin' me, all right."

The boys looked a bit edgy, watching him carefully from a distance of about six feet. Until last week, his threats had always worked, making kids cower in fear or simply run away. But now no one was running. The sight of him writhing on the floor of the cafeteria had weakened his game. Because Darrell had taken him down, others thought they could do it. Tyray could see it in their eyes. They were sizing him up.

"You ain't gonna do nothin'," Cedric barked. "Except maybe cry again." The four boys cackled loudly at Cedric's comment. Tyray's pulse throbbed in his neck.

"Stop laughin' or I'll take all y'all down," he screamed, spit flying from his mouth.

But they kept laughing. "It's broke. It's broke," Len said, dancing around in mock agony.

Tyray had to do something. He could not stand it anymore. With his good hand, he grabbed the kid closest to him, Cedric Hodden, and hurled him to the ground. "You like that?" he yelled, turning to challenge the other boys. "I got more where that come from."

Cedric scrambled to his feet and brushed the dirt off his jeans. "Man, I'd whup you bad, only I don't fight crippled people with busted hands. I ain't a punk like you."

"Let's teach this punk a lesson," Len said. "I'm tired of him runnin' off at the mouth." At once, the four boys closed in, cautious to avoid Tyray's good hand. As they circled, they snickered with excitement, unnerving Tyray. If they had been ganging up on him with anger, it might have been easier to bear, but they did not even respect him enough to take him seriously. He had become a joke, a fool. He had become a nothing.

Len and Eddie grabbed Tyray, hooking his arms behind his back. Together, Cedric and Shamar yanked off his jacket. Tyray struggled to free himself, but together, the four boys were stronger.

"Throw it up there, on the roof of that building," Eddie said.

"Get off of me!" Tyray growled, but he was powerless in their grip.

Cedric grabbed the arm of Tyray's jacket and tossed it onto a nearby roof, but it fell back to the ground. "Try again," urged Eddie, standing behind him.

"Get off!"

Tyray's mouth was completely dry. His heart raced, and his muscles trembled and strained, but he could not escape. At one point, he managed to free his leg and kick Len in the chest, but the boys overpowered him. As he struggled, Tyray remembered how he once tossed a kid's T-shirt into a toilet during gym class. The boy had cried like a baby while others laughed. Tyray could almost see the boy's face as he watched Cedric fling his jacket into the air.

On his second try, Cedric was successful. The jacket snagged on a jagged brick near the apartment roof and hung there. The boys released Tyray, shoving him to the ground and applauding Cedric's throw.

Tyray landed on the asphalt with a thud, partially rolling on his cast. A jolt of pain shot into his arm like a hot knife, causing him to wince.

"Look at him," Len roared. "He's gonna cry!"

"How's it feel to get paybacks?" Shamar laughed.

An old woman peered from an apartment window just below where Tyray's jacket hung. "What's the matter with you boys? What kinda fools are you, throwing clothes on my roof? You all need a good thrashin'. Now get outta here. If you don't stop your hollerin' and fightin', I'll get the cops after you, I swear I will!"

The boys scattered, leaving Tyray alone on the ground holding his wrist, his face covered in a layer of dirt and sweat. Tyray imagined how pitiful he looked lying on the ground holding his wrist, his jacket dangling from the roof like the carcass of a dead animal. For a moment, Tyray sat in silence, anger swirling in his chest like flames from a wind-driven fire.

But anger was not the only emotion Tyray felt. Somewhere deep inside, he also felt a knot of sadness and shame. Years ago, his father taught him there was no room for such feelings, that men were not supposed to cry. It was a lesson Tyray practiced every day. Forcing back bitter tears that threatened to gather in his eyes, Tyray stood up and brushed the dirt from his clothes.

In the distance, he heard the squeak of an old bicycle approaching. Turning quickly towards the sound, he recognized the figure on the bike even though he was at the other end of the block. It was Darrell Mercer.

Darrell biked towards Tyray for an instant but then quickly turned up an adjacent street out of sight. In seconds, the sound of the bike was gone. Tyray knew Darrell worked at a nearby grocery store. He wondered if he was on his way to work. Or maybe Darrell heard about what happened and decided to come to laugh at him too.

"Too late, Mercer," Tyray said bitterly. He looked up at his jacket and saw that the old woman continued to watch him.

Tyray felt even more humiliated standing in his undershirt beneath the old woman's gaze. There was no way he would go home without his jacket. If he did, his father would punish him. The jacket was relatively new, and Dad did not take kindly to clothes being lost or ruined.

"Whatcha starin' at me for?" Tyray shouted. "Just throw down my jacket."

The woman scowled and shouted back, "Don't you be givin' me orders, you fresh-mouthed thing. From what I've seen, you best not be givin' orders to nobody. Now you show me some respect, and I might be able to help you," she said.

Tyray lowered his head in frustration. The sadness in his chest seemed overwhelming. Never had things been this bad. Now even old people were disrespecting him.

"Please, lady, I just need to get my jacket so I can get outta here," Tyray muttered.

The woman went back into her apartment and returned with a broom, which she used to reach the jacket. After a few seconds, she managed to dislodge it, and the jacket tumbled to the ground with a thud. Tyray raced over to where it fell and put it on quickly. Eager to get away from the old woman, he left without a word.

"Kids today," she grumbled as he walked away.

Tyray was in a hot sweat when he reached his street. His mission now had even greater urgency. There was no way things could be right until he got a gun. Though he would terrorize Shamar, Len, Eddie and Cedric with it, his first target would be Darrell Mercer. He was the one who had caused Tyray to lose respect. He was the one who made it unsafe for Tyray to walk in his own neighborhood.

Of course, Tyray would not kill Darrell. He would just scare him, make him cower, make him beg, cry, and whimper. And if something happened, if a mistake occurred and Darrell got hurt, that was okay too.

Darrell had to pay.

When Tyray got home, his father was waiting.

"Where you been? Where you get off comin' home this late? Whatcha been doin' all afternoon, huh?" Dad threw questions at Tyray like swift punches.

"I been lookin' for work," Tyray said.

Dad grabbed his son's shirt front and shoved him against the wall. "Liar! No-good liar! If you been lookin' for work, tell me who you talked to."

"Uh, the guy . . . the guy in the pizza place," Tyray stammered.

"What guy? What pizza place?" Dad thundered.

Tyray searched his mind frantically. He pulled a name out of nowhere, knowing if he mentioned a real place, Dad would check. "Pop's Pizza place," he said.

"I never heard of no such place. Where is it?" Dad demanded. "Tell me where it is, boy."

"I . . . I don't remember," Tyray said.

"Liar!" Dad shouted, still clutching Tyray's shirt. Dad raised Tyray's face until it was just inches from his, "You tell me the truth!"

"All right," Tyray said in a shaky voice, "I was just hangin' out with some dude, shootin' hoops and stuff."

"Oh yeah? You got chores to do around here, and you waste time messin' with your friends? Your grades are slidin', and you're out all day shootin' hoops?"

"Dad, it's Saturday," Tyray pleaded.

"Don't you talk back to me, boy. I know what happens on these streets, especially to kids like you who don't have no sense. Now, you listen real close. The next time you go out, you tell me where you're goin' or you won't see sunshine for a while. And another thing. If the next report card ain't a whole lot better than the last one, you gonna get a beatin' you'll never forget, you hear what I'm sayin'?" Dad said, shaking Tyray for emphasis.

"Yeah, Dad," Tyray muttered.

With that, Dad pushed him away as if Tyray disgusted him so much he could not stand to see his face. Tyray hurried to his room and flopped down on the bed. Staring up at the water-stained ceiling, Tyray wiped his eyes, trying to fight off the tears that were gathering. Nearly ten years had passed since Tyray had really cried.

He was about five years old then. It was a bitter winter evening, and sleeting rain was pelting the front window when Tyray found a stray black puppy crouched against the house. Tyray wrapped the puppy in his jacket and brought it inside. Mom wanted to let Tyray keep the puppy, but Dad snatched it up and tossed it back into the wet cold and slammed the door after it.

"Don't need no stinkin' animal clut-terin' up the house," Dad had growled. *"We already got enough people livin' here, and enough bills to pay."*

That night, Tyray lay awake for hours hearing the cries of the whimper-ing puppy mix with the crash of rain and wind. By morning, a thin layer of ice had formed on the roofs of buildings. Tyray went looking for the puppy. He did not find it for three days, and he only found it then because of the smell. That had been the last time Tyray really cried, and that was over a dead, muddy bundle of fur in a dirty alley.

"It's gonna be all right, little man," Warren had said when he spotted Tyray leaning over the lifeless body.

Pushing the memory from his mind, Tyray folded his arms over his chest and resolved not to cry.

He hated feeling so weak. He hated Bluford and all its students and teach-ers. He hated Darrell Mercer and what he had done to his life.

And that night, for the first time ever, Tyray hated himself.

Chapter 4

Could things get any worse? Tyray wondered. It did not seem possible.

Tyray lay on the bed so full of anger that he could hardly keep his body still. And he felt near ready to explode. The only thing that gave him comfort was the idea that it was all going to change. As soon as he got a gun.

Just then there was a soft rap on Tyray's door. "Tyray?" Mom called out from the hall.

"Whadya want?" Tyray moaned, refusing to get up from his bed.

"May I come in, honey?"

Tyray rolled his eyes. It angered him when his mother treated him like a child. Reluctantly, Tyray swung his legs over the side of the bed, got up, and let her in. "Whadya want?" he repeated. "I got stuff to do, and I need to concentrate."

"I'm just worried about you, Tyray. You seem real unhappy," Mom said. "I don't like to see my baby like that."

"I'm fine," Tyray said. "Don't worry about me, Mom."

"You sure? Because if there's something you need to talk about, I'm here."

"I got nothin' to say," Tyray replied, looking down.

"Honey, I love you. You know that. I'd do anything in the world for you," Mom said, moving slowly towards the door.

"Don't call me honey, okay?" Tyray muttered.

Mom reluctantly left the room, and Tyray almost felt sorry for her. She was just as scared of Dad as he was. Yet she stood by Dad, allowing him to rule the family even when she knew he was wrong.

When Tyray was a boy, he watched from a darkened hallway as his father yelled at her. *"You don't sweet-talk no one, you understand me, woman?"* Dad fumed.

Mom whimpered. Tyray looked closer and saw that his father had her by the hair, and every time he wanted to make a point, he gave her a sharp yank.

"You don't sweet-talk no butcher, no fool come around sellin' insurance, nobody, understand?" Another, harder

yank. Mom's head jerked back. This time she did not even whimper.

"You're my woman, understand? I don't want no mess from you," Dad said with a final yank of her hair.

"Gil, I never did anything for you to be jealous about. Never," Mom cried.

Dad slapped her then. It had been many years ago, but Tyray could still hear the slap. Mom fell with the force of the blow, and Tyray remembered sucking in his breath. He waited to see what Mom would do. Would she grab a frying pan and whack Dad over the head? Grab her things and take Tyray and Warren to Grandma's house? He waited for her to do something. But she did nothing. The next morning she made fried eggs and bacon just the way Dad liked them, as if nothing had happened.

Tyray hated his father for that slap. And part of him hated his mother too for not doing anything, and for allowing him to slap Tyray countless times. Sure, she was scared of Dad. Tyray knew that. But she should have done something, Tyray thought. Anything.

On Monday morning, the phone rang before Tyray left for school. Mom answered it. "That was Mrs. Hodden," she said. "She wanted to apologize for what her grandson did Saturday."

Tyray felt his face burn hot with shame. "I don't know what she talkin' about," he said bitterly, struggling to maintain a few shreds of pride in front of his mother. "She just talkin' crazy. I heard that lady drinks all day, so she probably all drunk or somethin'."

"She said four boys grabbed you, and her grandson was one of them—"

"Shut up!" Tyray screamed, clamping his hands over his ears. Then he closed his eyes and struggled to calm down. His mind raced with images and sounds—Darrell Mercer's face, Cedric's laughter, his jacket being torn off him and thrown into the air, his father's booming voice.

His mother stared at him, her expression a mixture of sadness and concern. Just seeing her made him feel worse. He felt as if the entire world were somehow trying to insult him. Without a word, he rushed out. All that kept his feet moving was the gun. Once he had it, everything would get better, Tyray reassured himself as he made his way to Bluford.

After school, Tyray resumed his search. He went down to 43rd Street and found Jupiter James, Londell James's younger brother. If anyone had a gun, it would have to be the James brothers. Londell always seemed to have guns around. And from what Tyray heard in the neighborhood, Jupiter was following in his big brother's footsteps.

"Hey, whassup?" Tyray greeted Jupiter, trying to appear cool.

Though they had spoken a few times before, Tyray knew a lot about Jupiter. His mom dealt drugs, and his father had been stabbed to death in a dispute over stolen goods. Londell served time in prison for attempted murder, and Jupiter already had a rap sheet a mile long. Tyray had hassled people for years, but it was mostly kid stuff compared to what the Jameses did. But all that was about to change.

"Whatcha want, boy?" Jupiter barked, eyeing Tyray warily.

"Uh . . . I'm Tyray Hobbs," he stammered, his voice cracking slightly.

"So?" Jupiter said. "Am I suppose to know you or somethin'?"

"I'm lookin' for a gun," Tyray blurted, feeling foolish.

"What makes you think I'm the local arsenal, fool?" Jupiter asked.

Tyray hesitated. Up until a week ago, no one spoke to him in such a way, no one except his father. For an instant, Tyray wondered if he could overpower Jupiter and steal a gun from him. The two were nearly the same size. But then Tyray remembered Jupiter's reputation and his own broken hand. Now was not the time to fight.

"With your brother and all," Tyray began, "I just—"

"I ain't my brother," Jupiter scowled. "And I don't know you. Maybe you're workin' with the cops, tryin' to bust me."

"No. I just need a gun."

"What for?" Jupiter asked, a sneer on his lips. "You looking to join a gang? 'Cause you look more like a Boy Scout to me."

"Naw," Tyray said, swallowing hard and trying to ignore Jupiter's comment. "I got a score to settle. Some guys at school are hasslin' me, and I need to protect myself."

Jupiter glared at Tyray for several seconds before he finally spoke. "Know what, bro? You scare me. You got a psycho look in your eyes."

"Look, I need a gun and I need one now. You gotta help me. This one guy at school, he took me down, and now the whole school is doggin' me."

Jupiter paused thoughtfully. "Lemme look around. You know it's gonna cost you."

"How much?"

"Fifty," Jupiter said, "and that's only for a cheap gun. Nothin' fancy."

"Fifty?" Tyray groaned. It was the same price Bones had mentioned. In all the excitement to get a gun, Tyray forgot about the money he would need to pay for it. He wouldn't admit it to Jupiter, but he only had about two dollars to his name.

"Yeah, you figuring to get a gun for chump change, boy?" Jupiter asked in a nasty voice. "If you want a gun for a few bucks, go to the toy store."

"No, no, I ain't complainin'," Tyray said quickly. He just did not yet know where he would get the money.

"Don't waste my time unless you got the cash," Jupiter growled, turning away quickly.

"I'll get the money and I'll be back," Tyray said. Jupiter did not acknowledge Tyray's response. Instead, he strolled away in silence.

Tyray knew jokes about him continued to circulate throughout Bluford. In English class, students quietly laughed at him until Mr. Mitchell arrived. Tyray stewed in anger as the class began and sat almost motionless for the entire fifty minutes of the period. Instead of taking notes or answering questions, he drew sharp angular designs onto a blank page of his notebook.

"Can I talk to you for a minute, Tyray?" the teacher asked at the end of class. Tyray rolled his eyes as students rushed out of the classroom. Mr. Mitchell was one of the most well-liked teachers at Bluford. He was sharp too. Hardly anything got past him. When Tyray taunted Darrell, Mr. Mitchell was the only one who caught him in the act. And he was also nosy, Tyray thought, intruding into students' lives when he thought they needed help. He had done this with Darrell, and Tyray was sure he was going to try it with him. He had no time for the nosy teacher's charity.

"What for?" Tyray challenged. "I didn't do nothin'."

"A lot has happened to you in the last couple of weeks. How are you doing with everything?" Mr. Mitchell asked.

"I'm fine," Tyray replied, his face burning in anger and frustration. He wanted to scream *none of your business*, but instead he added, "My wrist is healing up good. The doctor says I can get the cast off in four weeks."

"That's great," Mr. Mitchell said, pausing briefly. "Listen, I know that was a pretty rough experience you went through. If someone's making it difficult for you—"

"Everything's cool," Tyray replied abruptly, leaning back in the chair and staring at his cast. How could he explain that everything—and everyone—was making his life miserable? *You don't know jack about me and you never will,* he wanted to say.

"Tyray, look," Mr. Mitchell said, "I know you're hurting, and I just want you to know that I've been there. I've been right where you are now. When I was your age I built a wall around myself, too. A lot of guys do that because they believe that it's the manly way. But it's not. The manly way is to admit that you've got things tearing you up on the inside. That's what being a man means. It's not about hiding your feelings and being angry at everyone. It's about dealing with

53

them so that you can be stronger than you used to be."

Tyray resented Mr. Mitchell. He had no right to poke and prod him. Yes, things were difficult. And yes, he was hurting on the inside. But Tyray had survived all his life without Mr. Mitchell telling him how to live. He was not about to spill his guts to a man wearing a Tweety Bird tie.

But as much as Tyray did not want to admit it, Mr. Mitchell had struck a nerve. Tyray felt a rush of sadness, one which took all his concentration to push back. He could not pour his heart out to Mr. Mitchell. He could not fall to pieces right there in the classroom. He was not that weak.

"You're not in a good place at all, Tyray," Mr. Mitchell added when he did not reply.

Tyray jerked forward in the chair, swallowing his emotions. "What you talkin' 'bout, Mr. Mitchell? I ain't had no more detentions. I'm doin' good."

"Oh sure, you've been staying out of trouble, and that's great," Mr. Mitchell said. "But you're torn up on the inside. I know how the guys have been riding you. I see what's going on. But look, you can get through this and come out the other side a stronger, better kid. You can make a fresh start. You'll be surprised how things can turn around once people see you're making an honest effort to change."

Yeah, right. Wait until you see how I change things, Tyray thought, imagining the feel of the gun in his hands. He forced a fake smile and said, "You're right, Mr. Mitchell. I'll try changin'. I've already decided to spend more time studyin'."

"Maybe you want to join a sport like wrestling. It did a world of good for Darrell Mercer. I know Coach Lewis would welcome you on the squad once your wrist heals," Mr. Mitchell said.

Tyray boiled at the mention of Darrell's name. There was no way he would spend a second with the kid who ruined his reputation, except to get revenge. Again, he swallowed hard before speaking.

"I'll think about it, Mr. Mitchell. Maybe I'll even talk to Mercer about it," Tyray said, smiling coldly as he pictured his future confrontation with Darrell. "Right now I'm spendin' a lotta time studyin', tryin' to bring up my grades and stuff, so I ain't got much time for sports."

"Tyray, you gotta get that chip off your shoulder, okay?" the teacher said, studying Tyray's face as if he were looking for a clue to a mystery.

"If you say so, Mr. Mitchell," Tyray replied. "But, believe me, I ain't got problems with nobody. I'm just mindin' my own business."

"Okay Tyray," Mr. Mitchell sighed. "If you ever need somebody to talk to, I'm here, okay?"

Tyray stood up and walked out of the classroom wearing a phony grin. He did not need to talk with Mr. Mitchell. What he needed was fifty dollars, and he needed it fast.

Chapter 5

After leaving Mr. Mitchell's room, Tyray spotted Lark walking alone in the hallway, clutching a small purse. When Tyray saw her, an idea struck him. Maybe she could help him find some money.

"Hey, Lark," he called out, trying to sound friendly.

"Hi, Tyray," she said, beaming.

Tyray fell in step beside her. "How you doin', girl?"

"I'm good," Lark said with a smile. Tyray could tell she was flattered by his attention. "How about you?" she asked.

"Not so good."

"What's wrong?" Lark asked, obvious concern on her face.

"I'm broke," Tyray began. "My mom's birthday is comin' up, and I wanted to buy her this nice necklace. But I can't afford it. Mom's been under a lot of pressure lately with my aunt bein' sick and all. I just thought the necklace would cheer her up, you know."

"That's such a sweet idea," Lark said. "It's a shame you don't have the money."

Tyray sensed his plan was working. "Maybe I'll be able to get it for her next year," he sighed. "If I'd only started saving sooner."

Lark was quiet for a while. Then she said, "You know what, Tyray? I've saved some money from baby-sitting, and I could lend it to you for your Mom's present."

"For real?" Tyray asked, acting surprised. "You sure? I don't feel right takin' your money. I could just get the present next year."

"No, I'm serious. You're being so sweet. I'd love to help your mom get her present."

"Girl, you're *all that*," Tyray said, draping his arm on her shoulder. "Mom's gonna be so happy. The necklace costs eighty dollars, but I already saved thirty. All I need is fifty more."

"That's a lot of money," Lark answered, seeming stunned.

"I know it, girl." Tyray said, trying his best to work his charm. "Why don't you just forget about it. I'll just get the necklace next year."

"No. I'll have fifty dollars after I babysit this weekend. You can borrow it."

"You sure?"

"Yeah," Lark said, looking up at him. "I want to help."

"Thanks, girl. You more than all right." Tyray caressed Lark's soft cheek with the back of his hand. "I'll pay you back as soon as I can." With those words, he turned and strolled to his next class, thrilled with the knowledge that he was getting closer to the gun.

When Tyray got home from school, his mother was cooking dinner. On days she came home early, Mom went to a lot of trouble making delicious meals. The living room was often filled with the aromas of pork chops, pot roasts, or fried chicken. She even made fresh salads and homemade pies, careful to roll the crusts herself so they would be perfect. Tyray never understood why his mother went to such great lengths. Dad rarely did anything but complain, no matter what she did.

Tyray eyed his mother as she worked in the hot kitchen. "What are you looking at, sweetie?" she asked when she noticed him. "You wondering if this pie will be done by dinnertime? Yes, it will. It'll bake up nice by then. Just the way your father likes it."

Tyray looked at his mother as if she were from another planet. He could not stand how Dad ruled over the house and how Mom allowed it to happen. What did she see in his father? Why did she live this way? Tyray knew that she got pregnant with Warren when she was just seventeen and Dad had married her right away. At the time, she dropped out of high school and never went back to finish. That was why she was now stuck in a low-paying job as an aide in a nursing home.

"How come you married him, Mom?" Tyray asked bluntly.

"What?" Mom exclaimed, nearly dropping the bowl of salad she had been carrying. "Why are you askin' me a question like that? I married your father because I loved him, and I still do."

"But how could you love him?" Tyray asked, surprised at his own honesty.

"Honey, what's wrong with you? Your daddy is a good man. He's working hard right now to take care of you, bustin' his back every day. Lotta men don't do that," she said defensively and then hesitated. "I know he's hard on you sometimes, but it's 'cause he worries. Ever since Warren went to jail, your father has never been the same."

Tyray did not want to hear his mother's excuses. Dad had been bullying the household for as long as he could remember, though it was true he had gotten much worse after Warren got arrested. Since then Dad seemed eager to get into an argument, and even the smallest thing would send him into a tantrum.

Watching his mother working hard in the kitchen, Tyray was filled with bitterness, and for once he could not hold it back. "Mom, you take too much from him," Tyray said bluntly. He had felt this way for years, but until now he had never said anything, not even to Warren. But the misery of the past week had changed him somehow, and he could barely control his words.

"Tyray, I won't have you talking that way about your father. He's a good man. He provides for us so we have a decent place to live and good food on the table. He ain't never cheated on me, and he loves you boys," Mom said.

"Mom, he don't love me. Not one bit. All he wants to do is push me around," Tyray said bitterly. "And I've seen him pull your hair and slap you in your face," he confessed. Never before had he told his mother he had seen what happened.

Mom stepped back and turned away from him, as if his words hurt her. "When did you see such a thing?"

"When I was in fifth grade," Tyray said, "and it was hot and I couldn't sleep—"

"Yes, that happened," Mom said, swallowing hard. "But it only happened that one time," she continued, her voice trembling. "Your father had been drinking, and he had a jealous fit. When he sobered up, I told him that if he ever laid a hand on me again I would take you and Warren to my mother's house and get a divorce. He's never hit me again, never. I swear that's true, Tyray."

Tyray looked into his mother's eyes, unsure how to respond. "Whatever," he sighed, shrugging. Then he went to his room.

Tyray wished Warren was still home. Warren was three years older than Tyray, and the two had always been very close. When Tyray was in kindergarten, he began to idolize his older brother. Back then, Warren let Tyray hang out with him and his older friends. But all that changed when Warren became a teenager. Then he did everything he could to keep Tyray from trailing him.

"Get lost, willya?" Warren would yell. *"Me and my boys don't need some little kid runnin' behind us, okay?"* Once Warren even took the wheels off Tyray's bike so he could not follow him. Another time, Warren locked Tyray in the bathroom so he and his friends could get away. Tyray was stuck there for two hours until Mom came home.

During his junior year in high school, Warren became a totally different person. His grades dropped, he became disrespectful, and he got into trouble left and right. One night, Warren and his friends held up a grocery store. The police caught Warren with a loaded gun. He was arrested and sentenced to three years in jail.

Mom and Dad were devastated by what happened, and Tyray was shattered. He still idolized his brother, no matter how much Warren had changed. Mom and Dad never let Tyray visit Warren in prison, but he was allowed to write him. The two had exchanged letters for a while, but it had been nearly six months since Tyray heard anything from Warren.

Tyray kept his brother's letters in a box under his bed. Alone in his bedroom, he reached down, grabbed the box, and pulled out the small stack of letters. Tyray flipped through the wrinkled white sheets of paper covered with Warren's angular print. He stopped at a letter Warren sent him late last year and read it.

Tyray,

How you holding up? How are Mom and Pops? I know they are angry at me for everything, and I don't blame them one bit. I'm trying to stay positive in here, but it ain't easy. I still got two years to go, and sometimes I don't think I can stand another day in here. I got three things that keep me from going crazy—weightlifting, books, and you.

I keep thinking about the bad example I set for you. I made mistakes, little brother. I played into the game that says you *gotta be tough, you gotta be the baddest dude around, you gotta show it off. But respect ain't about scaring others, and it ain't about having the right shoes or the best clothes. Sitting behind these bars, you see how all that stuff is a lie. I'd give anything to be with you on the outside again. There ain't no respect in prison. Whatever you do, don't end up like me. Don't play the game I played. Stay straight, do your best in school, and don't let Dad get to you. I'll be writing again soon.*

Peace,

Warren

Tyray folded the letter and placed it back inside the box. He wondered when he would see Warren again. Around the time his brother began dabbling in crime, Tyray started making some discoveries of his own. He noticed how smaller kids were intimidated by him, how they looked at him nervously. Tyray liked the feeling that gave him. Up until then, it was Tyray who was always afraid. Afraid of Dad who acted like an angry giant. Afraid of Warren who was older and stronger. Afraid of Warren's friends, strangers like Bones who carried guns into his brother's room.

It was not long before Tyray discovered kids would do stuff for him just to stay on his good side. Some would even try to earn his friendship by acting mean towards other kids. They treated him as if he were someone important. They showed him respect. But Darrell Mercer changed all that. Now Tyray was back to being a nobody.

But not for long.

As Tyray approached Bluford the next morning, he spotted Darrell standing outside the front doors of the high school. He seemed to be waiting for someone.

Tyray glared at Darrell, holding back an urge to pound the boy on the Bluford steps. But to his surprise, Darrell stared at him and smiled slightly. Tyray froze. Was Mercer going to rub it in a little more?

"Tyray, we gotta talk," Darrell said, taking a deep breath. "I know some guys are giving you a hard time, and that ain't right."

Tyray scowled. So that was it, he thought. Ruining his reputation was not enough. Now Mercer wanted to show everyone at Bluford he was a bigger man than Tyray.

"Boy, get out of my face!" Tyray growled through clenched teeth.

Darrell took a step back. "What's your problem?" he sputtered. "We don't have to be enemies forever, do we?"

"I hate you, Mercer," Tyray said coldly. "And I'm gonna pay you back. One day soon, you're gonna wish you never left Philadelphia."

Darrell's smile vanished, instantly replaced by a look of worry.

Tyray nodded in satisfaction. Darrell was under a cloud of fear again. It was the way things were in the beginning. And it was the way they would stay, Tyray thought, turning away from Darrell and storming into Bluford.

Chapter 6

At lunchtime, Tyray saw Amberlynn Bailey and Jamee Wills talking to Lark. She was sitting at a table alone, and the two girls were standing on either side of her. Quietly, he approached the girls from behind so he could eavesdrop.

"Lark, don't give him any money," Jamee was saying. "That boy is no good."

"That's right," Amberlynn chimed in. "The only reason he needs money is 'cause people like Darrell aren't payin' him anymore. If he's so broke, tell him to get a job."

"I bet he ain't even gonna use the money to buy a present for his mom," Jamee added. "He's probably after something for himself."

"I don't believe Tyray is lying to me," Lark said.

"Believe it, girl," Jamee said, putting her hands on her hips. "That boy—"

Jamee turned and spotted Tyray through the corner of her eye. All three girls looked at him awkwardly. He glared at Jamee.

"We'll catch up with you later, Lark," Amberlynn said, leading Jamee away from the table. Tyray noticed they were careful to avoid looking at him directly.

"Tyray, are you really buying a present for your mom?" Lark asked. "Tell me the truth."

"Girl, I told you. I'm buyin' her this necklace I saw at the mall. I know it'll cheer her up. He paused and looked at her. "It's okay if you don't believe me. I'm used to people not trustin' me. The whole school's down on me right now. I don't blame you if you hate me too."

"Oh Tyray, I don't hate you. I really like you," Lark said, placing her hand gently on Tyray's arm.

Tyray wondered whether Lark really believed him. Glancing at the tiny scar on her lip, he suddenly felt uncomfortable. There was something vulnerable about Lark. She reminded him of the abandoned puppy from years earlier.

"My friends are always looking out for me," Lark said. "They think I'm too trusting, but that's just the way I am.

You haven't given me any reason not to trust you, right?"

Inside, Tyray cringed. Lark's comments made him feel dirty. But he could not allow anything to come between him and a gun.

"Whole school hates me," Tyray said. "If I dropped dead, they'd all celebrate. Amberlynn and Jamee would be throwin' that party. They'd have the biggest celebration of all."

"They don't hate you, not exactly." Lark replied.

"Yeah, well they don't know jack 'bout me! Everybody always talkin' 'bout me and gettin' in my business, and they don't know nothin'. I don't care what they say." Tyray fumed as he sat down next to Lark, watching her carefully. "Baby, why don't you just listen to 'em. Just walk away and forget about me," he added. Part of him meant the words, though he knew Lark would never do such a thing. Instead, she did exactly what he expected.

"No, no, I'm not going anywhere, Tyray," she said. "And you know what else? I have something for you and your mom." Lark reached into her pocket, pulled out two twenty-dollar bills, and handed them to Tyray. "I'll have ten more tomorrow," she said proudly.

"Girl, you're gonna make my momma so happy," Tyray said, quickly taking the money. "This is gonna be her best birthday present ever." Tyray put one arm around Lark and used the other to stuff the money in his shirt pocket.

A few minutes later, he was heading out of the cafeteria, excited that he was so much closer to purchasing the gun. Yet as Tyray walked away, the money felt heavy in his shirt pocket, like a bundle of guilt hanging directly over his heart.

At the end of the day, Tyray took the long way home from school, hoping he might run into Jupiter James. With Lark's forty dollars in hand, he thought Jupiter might cut the price and sell the gun to him right there.

Several younger guys hanging on the corner nodded to Tyray as he turned onto 43rd Street. Tyray knew the rules. No one would hassle him as long as he stayed cool. Trouble on this street would be bad for business, so everything was quiet. But Tyray didn't trust the silence, and he could feel many hidden eyes watching him from inside the buildings on both sides of the street.

"Hey, bro," Tyray asked a boy in a backward baseball cap, "Seen Jupiter around?"

"Juju?" the boy asked. "Nope. He's busy, man." The boy was thirteen or fourteen with a thin, angular face and bright black eyes.

"He ain't around?" Tyray asked again.

"Nah. His mom's sick, maybe dyin'," the boy said. "Jupiter's down at the hospital. Don't mess with him now, man."

Tyray nodded, trying to hide his disappointment. Jupiter was his best chance of getting a gun immediately. Without Jupiter, he had nowhere else to turn but to Bones. But Tyray did not feel like waiting until Friday.

"When's he comin' back?" Tyray asked, refusing to give up. "Maybe I'll catch up with him then."

"Don't nobody know," the boy said. He looked hard at Tyray. "Whatcha want, man? I might be able to hook you up."

"I need a gun," Tyray said bluntly. "Need one bad."

"For real?" the boy asked, his eyes growing bright with interest.

"Yeah?" Tyray asked. "Can you get me a gun tonight?"

"Maybe," the skinny kid said. "Come out to Muscleman Gym. Be there tonight, around eleven, okay? And bring the money."

"How much?" Tyray asked.

"Whatcha got?"

"Forty."

"That ain't much, man. Can only get you a cheap gun for that." The boy paused for a second as if he was planning something. "You be behind the gym. Eleven tonight," he said.

"You serious?" Tyray asked, his heart racing.

"Yeah," the boy said. "I'm straight up, bro. Just be there."

Tyray nodded and rushed home. He was so close to the gun now. He could almost feel its cold, heavy weight in the palm of his hand. The only obstacle now was his father. There was no way Dad would allow him out of the house at 11:00 on a school night.

At about 8:30, Tyray went to his bedroom, saying he was tired. Then he nervously watched the minutes pass by on his alarm clock. Periodically, he listened to hear if Dad was still watching TV. Tyray did not know how he'd get out of the house in time if his father stayed up late. Every so often, he heard the interrupted sounds of TV channels being changed. A shudder raced down Tyray's back as he imagined what his father would do if he found out about the gun.

When Warren was arrested, Tyray had hid in his bedroom as Dad rumbled through the house yelling and smashing things. *That boy is a disgrace to this family,* Dad screamed over and over again. At one point his father even said Warren was disowned.

Tyray was enraged that Dad had said such a thing, but he kept his thoughts to himself. Later he wondered if Warren was actually better off without his father threatening and punishing him. No matter what Dad said, Tyray vowed never to abandon his brother. His mom felt the same way, though they rarely mentioned Warren when Dad was around.

Once, Mom tried to explain that Dad was devastated by what had happened with Warren. But Tyray did not want to listen to her. All he heard was anger in his father's words. There was nothing else in the bitter man's heart, Tyray concluded.

"Don't let Dad get to you." Warren's words echoed in Tyray's mind.

"Yeah, right," Tyray said bitterly to himself. At 9:30, he listened as his father silently watched a sitcom. Every few minutes, Tyray heard canned laughter from the fake TV audience. At 10:00, the channel changed, and Tyray listened to the local news.

"Go to bed," Tyray whispered nervously as he watched the numbers change to 10:10 on his alarm clock. With six blocks to walk, Tyray knew he needed to leave his house by 10:50 at the latest in order to get to the gym by 11:00.

At 10:30, Tyray heard the TV click off and then the familiar thud of his father's heavy footsteps growing louder in the hallway. For a second, Tyray thought Dad was going to come into his bedroom. He closed his eyes tightly and pretended to be asleep. But then the steps faded, and Dad went into his bedroom and closed the door quietly.

For several moments, the house was silent, and all Tyray heard was the faint wail of a police siren somewhere in the distance. Tyray knew his Dad fell asleep quickly, so he prepared to leave. At 10:50, with the house dark and silent, Tyray crept quietly down the hallway and out the front door of his house, careful not to make a sound.

Chapter 7

The street outside was nearly deserted. A mottled cat hissed loudly from underneath a parked car as Tyray made his way out into the street. On a nearby corner, a few people stood outside a liquor store smoking cigarettes. Further down the block, Tyray spotted a guy pumping gas at a self-service station.

It was nearly 11:00. Tyray had to rush to get to Muscleman Gym on time. He started to jog, making sure the twenty-dollar bills in his pocket were secure. His fingers tingled as he got closer to the gym. Just a few more blocks and the gun would be his.

Then he saw a black and white police car in the distance. It was coming directly towards him.

For an instant, Tyray did not know what to do. If the police found him, they would surely take him home, and then his father would get him. Yet if he ran, the police would chase him, suspecting that he was running from a crime that he had just committed. Even if he tried to smooth-talk them, he would get in trouble for being out so late and breaking the city curfew for kids. They would also want to know why he had so much cash in his pocket at such a late hour. Tyray knew other kids in the neighborhood who were hassled by cops for much less. He knew he had to avoid the police.

Darting into a small alley, Tyray ducked behind a rusted old van. He could hear the police car slowly approaching. When it was across from the alley where he was hiding, the cruiser stopped. A second later, a bright spotlight shined into the alley, casting long shadows. Tyray squatted down as the light moved back and forth. A dog in a nearby apartment started to bark.

Tyray glanced at his watch. It was 11:00. Pinned in the shadow of the van, Tyray began looking for a way out of the alley. The only path he could see was through someone's backyard. Fortunately, the van blocked the view of the small fenced yard. Tyray was sure the officers in the cruiser could not see him or his possible escape route. He listened closely and heard male voices from the police car, followed by the sound of a police radio. He had to move. Now.

Bolting from behind the old van, Tyray grabbed the top of the shoulder-high fence and vaulted himself over it. In less than a second, he was in the unfamiliar backyard, stumbling over an old tire and some shrubs. The dog began to bark louder. Somewhere behind him, a light went on in an apartment window. Tyray jumped to his feet and sprinted around the house and into its front yard. Climbing over a metal fence, he rushed into the deserted street.

Following shadows and dark alleys, Tyray raced towards the gym, leaving the police car blocks behind him. On the way home, he would have to be more careful.

It was six minutes after eleven when Tyray arrived at the corner where two lanky trees scratched the sky. Muscleman Gym was just ahead. Tyray's knees wobbled with nervous energy as he approached the familiar stucco building with the red neon sign.

Tyray had been to the gym twice before, once a few years ago to watch his brother lift weights, and another time last summer when he was training for the Bluford football team. Those memories seemed distant now as he stood in the dark scanning the street for police cars.

Glancing at the building, Tyray saw that the lights inside were off, and he suspected the small gym had closed hours ago. Careful not to make a sound, he crept into an adjacent alley and waited. He hoped he wasn't too late.

A hazy mist hung in the air, distorting the distant streetlights. A dim halo encircled the amber moon, and no stars were visible. The night seemed strangely quiet as Tyray looked at his watch again. It was 11:10.

The longer Tyray waited, the more nervous he became. Could the boy have lied to him? Tyray glanced up and down the alley looking for movement, but nothing happened. The minutes dragged by with an agonizing slowness. At 11:15, Tyray was about to get up and leave when he heard a voice from the darkness.

"Down the alley, man," the voice said. It did not sound like the kid he had spoken to earlier, but that made sense, Tyray thought. That kid probably got someone else to handle the sale. As he walked down the alley alongside the gym, he still did not see anyone.

"Over here," another voice called out. "By the garbage dumpster."

Tyray walked over to a rusty metal dumpster. Stacked against both sides of the container were dozens of glistening trash bags and dirty cardboard boxes. The air was heavy with the stench of rotting food and spilled beer. Tyray covered his nose at the putrid odor. Through the corner of his eye, he noticed a sudden movement.

Two boys emerged from behind the dumpster, and a third came from a small doorway in the side of the building. Tyray turned in time to see a wooden stick being swung towards the back of his head.

CRACK!

The sound rocketed through Tyray's skull, and he was sent sprawling into a metal trash can. Overwhelmed by pain, he collapsed into the pile of trash bags, placing both hands over his head. A large rat scuttled by his face. Dazed, Tyray heard several people whispering and then felt a pair of hands frantically searching his pockets. Within seconds, the voices were gone, and there was silence.

For several long minutes, Tyray lay motionless as pain drove through his head. Slowly he managed to sit upright. It was then that he noticed his hands were bloody. Carefully he touched the painful knot where the stick hit him and discovered that he was bleeding.

Alarmed, Tyray staggered to his feet. His head throbbed, and he had to grab the wall of the gym to keep from falling down into the garbage again. Walking unsteadily away from the dumpster, Tyray reached into his pocket. It was empty.

"My money!" he yelled, forgetting his pain. He looked where he had fallen, hoping to find his cash lying amidst the debris. But all he found was more garbage.

"No!" he said stomping down on a beer can in frustration, his head still throbbing.

It was all a setup, he realized. The boy and his friends had lured him out just to rob him. It was as simple as that. Tyray closed his eyes and took three long, deep breaths. How could he have been so stupid? Now here he was, robbed and maybe even bleeding to death, and he had no one to blame but himself.

"No!" Tyray yelled again hoarsely, kicking several trash bags until they ripped open, spilling garbage on the ground.

Tyray slumped against a brick wall and grabbed his aching head. Every miserable event that happened in the last week and a half streamed through his mind. He relived his agony on the cafeteria floor, the lecture in the principal's office, the humiliation with Cedric Hodden, and now a robbery.

Despair clawed at his chest as he made his way home. He felt like a laughingstock, a fool, and nothing he tried to do allowed him to escape the humiliation. Tyray felt trapped in a cold, dark tunnel with no way out.

As he slowly neared his home, Tyray considered his options. He could not call the police, but he could return to Jupiter's street in the daylight and find the boy who had set him up. But he knew the kid would just deny what happened. *"I looked for you, but you never came last night,"* he would say. Then he would probably laugh at Tyray like everybody else. *"Why don't you call the po-leeece? Tell them cops you wanted to buy a cheap gun offa me and you got robbed instead. See how that flies,"* the boy would say.

Tyray gave up that idea fast. He reached his house and went slowly up the stairs, exhausted and in pain. He knew he should see a doctor, but that was impossible. How could he explain to his father what he had been doing out on the street at that hour? When Dad got through with him, a cut on his head would be the least of his worries.

Cautiously he crept inside the house and tiptoed down the hallway to his room. He was grateful that his parents' bedroom door was closed as he stepped into his room. At least he would not have to deal with them. Silently, he pulled off his clothes and climbed into bed, careful not to brush his tender scalp.

Staring into the blackness of his bedroom, Tyray wished he could just go to sleep and never wake up. It was not that he wanted to die. He just wanted to stop what was happening. Yet he could see no end to it.

The sadness Tyray fought pressed heavily on his chest. Everything he knew no longer seemed to work. Kids were not afraid, and he was unable to force his will on others. Worse was an overwhelming emotion Tyray tried to deny, one his father taught him was only for weaklings. It was a feeling Tyray had seen for years on the faces of skinny kids who needed teachers for protection. It was fear, and Tyray hated himself for feeling it.

Turning his light on, Tyray grabbed a pen and a sheet of notebook paper. He wanted to speak to his brother, to get his advice, and to hear his voice. Quickly he began drafting a letter.

> *Warren,*
>
> *I'm in trouble. You said I could talk to you about anything, so that's what I'm doing. There's a lot going on here at school and at home. Dad keeps pushing me, and I can't take it. But there is other stuff too. I know if you were here, you'd understand. I'm trying to get myself out of a mess. I'm not sure what to do. I am thinking about . . .*

Tyray stopped and looked at his words. They seemed desperate, scratched into the lined paper in a messy scrawl. Frustrated, Tyray crumpled the paper into a ball and tossed it into his trash can.

There was only one way to get back the respect he lost. He had to beat everyone at their game. He had to get back at Rodney and Cedric and Len. But he would start with Darrell. It was the only way. If it was the last thing he did, Tyray had to take Darrell down.

Tyray woke up the next morning with a fierce headache. His pillowcase was stained with dried blood from his head wound. With his bedroom door still closed, Tyray yanked off the bloody pillowcase and buried it in his bedroom trash can. Luckily the pillow itself was not stained, and Tyray found a clean pillowcase so his mother would not notice anything unusual.

Taking a shower, Tyray carefully washed the blood from his hair. He watched the rust-colored water pool briefly at his feet and then vanish down the drain. Tenderly Tyray touched the wound on the back of his head. There was a hard knot just above and behind his left ear. The lump contained a gash the size of his thumbnail. He was glad to discover that the cut was not deep and that it was nearly invisible under his hair.

"Hi, honey," Mom said when Tyray came to breakfast.

He did not have much of an appetite, but he decided to eat two pieces of toast so his parents would not suspect anything unusual. His father was already finishing breakfast when Tyray entered the kitchen.

"Got a big job today. Got a coupla new guys startin' today, too. I'm gonna need to work 'em extra hard 'cause we're under a deadline," Dad said menacingly, getting up from the table. "Contract says if we take too long, money gets deducted from our profits. I ain't about to let that happen," he added, looking over at Tyray. "You studying so you get some decent grades, boy? I don't never want to see a report card like the last one you got."

"Yeah, I'm studyin'."

"You better keep your nose in them books," Dad snapped. "You gotta get yourself outta this house one day and make a life of your own. And you can't do it by bringing home C's and D's."

Tyray struggled not to roll his eyes at his father's words. Every once in a while, his father got on his case about school. To Tyray it was not that his father valued school. It seemed more that he just wanted another reason to yell at him.

"I'm gonna make some changes," Tyray said. "You'll see."

"You better, boy," Dad said, grabbing his jacket and heading out the door.

Tyray cursed under his breath and headed off to school.

Chapter 8

When he arrived at Bluford, Tyray learned that a pep rally had been scheduled in the gym for just before lunch. All freshmen were expected to attend. Tyray did not mind such events during football season, when he got to attend as an athlete. But this pep rally was for winter sports. That meant the wrestling team and Darrell Mercer would be included. The last thing he wanted to do was see people praise Darrell.

"We've had a great season this year," Coach Lewis said, talking about the wrestling team. "A couple of our seniors are going to the state championships. And from the looks of things, a number of our freshmen may be there one day too."

Tyray rolled his eyes. He would rather be in Mr. Fitch's history class. He listened as the coach praised several wrestlers and then mentioned the team's success in a recent match against Lincoln High.

"Each year the team selects an award for the most improved member on the team," the coach continued. Tyray's eyes widened. "This year's recipient is Darrell Mercer."

Tyray watched in horror as Darrell stood up and waved. Many kids in the bleachers clapped loudly, and a few even chanted, "Dar-rell, Dar-rell!"

Amberlynn Bailey and Jamee Wills squealed loudly at the news, and several guys on the wrestling squad patted Darrell on the back.

Tyray stood up. Each clap for Darrell was like an insult aimed directly at him, making his head throb even more. Desperate, Tyray spotted Mr. Mitchell sitting with his section of freshmen and mumbled, "Gotta go to the bathroom. I'm sick."

Mr. Mitchell nodded, and Tyray ran down the bleachers towards the hallway.

"Hard to take, Tyray?" Jamee jeered as Tyray descended the steps. "What goes around comes around."

Tyray made it to the bathroom and went inside. The room was empty, and

Tyray kicked a trash can, sending it smashing into a bathroom stall. His head ached, and he rubbed the wound repeatedly while listening for the end of the pep rally. Finally, after about ten minutes, the rally was over, and Tyray heard everyone leaving the gym. When he came out of the bathroom, Mr. Mitchell was standing there waiting for him.

"Feeling better, Tyray?" Mr. Mitchell asked.

"Yeah, I'm fine," Tyray said, turning to walk away. "Somethin' I ate, I guess."

"You're upset, aren't you?" Mr. Mitchell asked.

"I don't know what you're talkin' about, man," Tyray snapped.

"Kids are mean, Tyray. They're a lot like chickens. When chickens find one of the flock vulnerable, they peck it to death. Darrell was on the receiving end of the pecking a while ago, and now I think you're catching some of it. I know how tough it can be," Mr. Mitchell said.

"I don't know what you're talkin' about, Mr. Mitchell. I ain't no chicken. Look, I gotta get to class."

"Tyray, this will all pass," Mr. Mitchell added. "One day you're gonna realize that none of this is important.

But there are some things you can do right now to change things. You've got to own up to your part in this, and you gotta get that chip off your shoulder and reach out to the other kids."

"I ain't reachin' out to nobody. I ain't got problems. Don't waste no time on me, Mr. Mitchell," Tyray insisted, walking away from the teacher.

At lunchtime, Tyray approached Lark in the cafeteria.

She glanced up at him and then turned away. Tyray wondered what he would say if she asked him about the money. Would she give him more money if he asked for it?

"Hi, Lark," he said, sitting next to her. "Girl, you look good today."

Lark opened her can of soda but said nothing. She avoided eye contact with him. "Yesterday, I went with my friend Livvie to see her grandma in the nursing home where your mom works," she said. "Livvie's grandma is pretty sick."

"Too bad," Tyray said trying to figure out what Lark had to say.

Lark raised her gaze and looked right at him. "Your Mom was there, Tyray. We got into a conversation about birthdays.

Of course, I kept the necklace a secret. She told me she just celebrated her birthday two months ago," Lark said, taking a deep breath. "Have you been lyin' to me just to get my money?" she asked, tears in her eyes.

Tyray's heart sank. He glanced down to escape her gaze. "You . . . uh . . . I didn't really get her anything nice, so I thought I'd give it to her as a late present as soon as I could afford it," he explained.

"That's not what you told me before," Lark said, shaking her head, a look of disappointment on her face. "You said you wanted to get it for her this year. You acted like you had to get it soon. I told your mom we're friends at school, and she seemed real glad about that. I asked how your sick aunt was doing, and she said there wasn't anyone in the family that was sick. I didn't say anything else 'cause I didn't want to get you in trouble."

"She's lyin'," Tyray blurted out awkwardly. "Mom's like that. She don't like people knowin' her business."

"No, Tyray. I think *you're* the one who's lying," Lark replied. "Everyone kept telling me not to trust you, but I didn't listen. I kept hoping that they were wrong, that you were different from what they said. Well, I guess *I* was the one who was wrong."

Tyray's mind spun wildly as he searched for something to say. "Okay, okay. Do you really want the truth? The truth is that I . . . was embarrassed to tell you why I needed the money," Tyray said, thinking quickly.

Lark's eyes widened. "What is it?"

"I owe some guys a lot of money, and they said they're gonna hurt me if I don't pay. They did this to me last night," Tyray insisted, bending forward to show her the gash on the back of his head. "I still gotta get fifty dollars or they're gonna hurt me again. I didn't want to admit that to you."

"Tyray, they can't get away with something like that," Lark said. "You have to go to the principal and tell her what's happening."

"No, you don't understand. The principal hates me. She's just lookin' for a reason to kick me outta Bluford," Tyray said.

"Well, go to Mr. Mitchell. He'll help you. He's great about helping kids with problems," Lark suggested.

"Baby, you don't get it. If I bring anyone else into this, those guys are gonna make it worse for me. All I can do is pay them off. That's why I asked you for the money. You're my only hope."

"Tyray, I can't keep giving you money. I already gave you everything I had. I believed you when you told me about your Mom's present, and you were lying to me. How can I be sure that you're not lying to me right now? I don't know what to do." Lark's eyes began to water, and she wiped them with her fingers.

"Just walk away then," Tyray said bitterly, surprised at how much Lark's tears bothered him. "That's what everybody does. No reason you should be different."

"Tyray!" Lark sobbed.

He glanced up to see Jamee Wills coming towards them. Passing Tyray in icy silence, Jamee rushed to Lark's side and put her hand on her friend's shoulder. "Come over and eat with us, Lark. You don't have to stay here." Lark got up slowly. "Me and Amberlynn are gonna go to the mall after school. My sister is driving us. We want you to come too, Lark," Jamee said as they walked away.

"You need to mind your own business," Tyray snapped at Jamee.

"My friend *is* my business," Jamee shot back. "And it's my business when she gets mixed up with losers like you."

Jamee pulled Lark to a table on the far side of the cafeteria, where Amberlynn was sitting. Tyray knew by the look on Lark's face that she was confused. As he watched her wipe tears from her eyes, he experienced a twinge of guilt.

Tyray looked around and realized he was completely alone in the middle of the crowded cafeteria. *So this is how it's gonna be from now on,* he concluded. His only comfort had been the knowledge that he would soon have a gun. Tomorrow he would meet Bones as they had agreed to nearly a week ago. But without money, Bones would just laugh at him.

Just then, a light bulb turned on in Tyray's head. There was one place where he had not yet gone for money, a place with more risk then robbing a bank. His mother's money stash.

Mom had savings she called her 'cheat money.' Every payday she hid cash in her dresser drawer. When it grew to a nice sum, she would use it to take her mother to dinner or buy herself something she needed. Dad knew about the stash, and he often borrowed from it. Tyray knew if Dad found him taking money, he would be in the worst trouble of his life.

But he had to do something.

Mom's money was the only answer. As long as he returned it quickly and without Dad knowing, nothing bad would happen. Once he got the gun, Tyray figured he could start scaring kids. They would start paying him again, and he could replace Mom's cash before anyone knew it was gone. By then, everything would return to normal.

As soon as his final class ended, Tyray sprinted from Bluford, rushing to arrive home before his mother. He had about five minutes to spare when he walked into the house. Making sure no one was home, he went quickly into his parents' room. He cautiously opened the drawer and found the 'cheat money' hidden between two folded shirts. Tyray counted one hundred and twenty dollars. He took out fifty dollars and carefully arranged the clothes in the exact position he had found them. Unless Mom looked for the money immediately, there would be no way she would know what he had done.

Tyray's hands shook as he folded the bills and shoved them deep into the pocket of his jeans. Immediately, he felt dirty. He had done many bad things in his life that did not bother him, but this was different. He had never stolen anything from his mother.

Struggling to push the guilt from his mind, Tyray focused his thoughts on the gun. "My gun is gonna change everything," he whispered to himself, quietly fighting the images of Lark and his mother, which gently haunted him in the darkened bedroom.

When Tyray went to bed that night, he slept fitfully, tossing every few hours, unable to get comfortable. At one point, he dreamt of Lark's face. Tears were in her eyes. To his horror, Tyray realized she was sitting alone in a church pew crying. Before her was a coffin, and in it Tyray saw his own body, a gun resting on his chest.

Chapter 9

Friday at Bluford passed by in a blur. Tyray struggled through each class, waiting for the bell to ring so he would be one step closer to the end of the day.

At lunchtime, Lark sat with Jamee, and only once did Tyray see her glance in his direction. He also saw Darrell laughing with a group of kids. *Just wait*, he thought, feeling the weight of his mother's money in his pocket. *Just wait.*

After school, Tyray swiftly walked to the fast-food restaurant where he had run into Bones a week earlier. He never felt more eager. His arms shook with nervous energy, and his stomach felt uncomfortably tense. The smell of hamburger, which usually enticed him, now slightly nauseated him.

Without looking at anyone, Tyray climbed onto a stool at the counter and waited.

"Gimme a burger with the works," said a deep voice behind him. Tyray turned to face Bones, who had crept next to him.

"Hey, Bones," Tyray said softly, looking at the paper-thin skin stretching across the man's forehead.

Bones did not turn his head. For a second, Tyray thought Bones had not heard him. But then the skinny man spoke up. "You don't know me, boy. Remember that," he said under his breath.

Tyray nodded and looked away. He figured Bones did not want to be seen in public with someone he was selling a gun to. Tyray had seen other kids in the neighborhood act the same way when they were selling something illegal. Without a word, Tyray sat as Bones ate his burger and swallowed black coffee. Then Bones walked out onto the street. Tyray waited a few seconds before following him.

"You're learning, little brother," Bones said when Tyray met him in the alley around the corner. It stank of garbage. Bones began to cough violently, his chest heaving uncontrollably.

"You all right?" Tyray asked.

"No. I'm the walking dead, boy. I got lung cancer," Bones said.

Tyray looked up at Bones, stunned at his frankness. For an instant, he did not know what to say. It was true that Bones looked sick, but Tyray never figured it was that bad. "So . . . you gonna see a doctor or what?" Tyray finally said.

Bones coughed again, spitting something red onto the ground. Then he turned and looked into Tyray's face.

"You gonna kill somebody, ain't you? I can see it. When a man is fixing to kill somebody, he gets a funny look. Maybe it's the blood pumping. Maybe it's the fear."

Tyray stepped back, unsure how to respond. He just needed the gun. As long as he got the gun, he would say whatever the sick man wanted.

"I was about your age when I took out my first," Bones said, breaking the tense silence. "He had this baby face. He was young, yeah . . . funny . . . I don't remember the others, but I remember him. He was a bad dude, but he had this baby face, big, wide eyes like a cartoon. You remind me of him."

Just shut up and sell me the gun, Tyray thought, struggling to remain calm.

"I remember him when he was dying . . . the way his eyes went wild and his cheeks puffed out . . . the blood and all." Bones took a long hard look at Tyray and then shook his head. "You were just a little punk when I first met you. I always knew you were headed for trouble. Warren was always worried about you. He'd be all over me if he knew what I was doin'. Let's get this over with before I change my mind. You got the money?"

"Fifty bucks," Tyray said, handing over his mother's cash.

Bones counted the money slowly, straightening each bill. "I know I shouldn't sell you a gun, but I ain't stupid. If I don't sell it to you, some other fool will. And right now, I need the cash." Bones folded the bills and placed them in his jacket pocket.

"Boy, you got a choice to make. This ain't on my hands. If you take that dude out, his face is gonna be with you until the day you die. You'll know it better than you know your momma's face. Be the last face you see every night before you go to sleep. Be the last face you see before you die."

There was a long silence. "I'm sicka all you kids," Bones growled as he moved down the alley.

"What about my gun?" Tyray asked, his voice rising in alarm.

Bones turned slightly and pointed a skinny finger at a rusting metal dumpster. "Look for the white bag on top of the dumpster."

Tyray rushed to the dumpster and saw a small white bag perched on a pile of trash. Quickly he snatched up the bag and ripped into it. Inside was a small solid object wrapped tightly in newspaper. Tyray's hands were shaking so badly, he nearly dropped the bundle. Finally, after removing several sheets of newspaper, Tyray broke through to the object.

A small metal revolver rested in his palm.

Tyray looked up into the alley. Bones was gone. Stuffing the gun into his backpack, Tyray hurried towards home, his heart pounding wildly.

When Tyray got home, he tried to behave normally so his parents would not be suspicious. His mother's smile told him that she had not checked her room or noticed the missing money. Not yet.

After dinner, Tyray went to his room and locked the door behind him. He pulled the gun from his backpack and stared at it in the dim light of his bedroom, its dull metal the color of a school blackboard.

The gun was short and stubby, no bigger than Tyray's open hand. It almost seemed like a toy, except it was much heavier than any toy gun Tyray had played with as a child. It felt as if it was made of lead. Tyray raised the gun and pointed it. Seeing his shadow stretched out against his bedroom wall gave him a strange chill, and he turned away quickly.

The gun was the answer, Tyray insisted to himself.

He lifted the mattress of his bed and hid the gun underneath it. His mother never came into his room, and if she did, she would never look there. He lay back on the bed thinking about the gun hidden just below him.

It was time to start setting everything right.

On Saturday, Tyray hid the gun in his jacket and went to the apartment complex where Rodney Banks lived. Up until Darrell had his moment in the cafeteria, Tyray and Rodney hung out together on Saturday afternoons. Soon everything would go back the way it was. Very soon.

Tyray spotted Rodney shooting baskets with a younger boy. Quickly he approached them.

"Banks, we gotta talk," he shouted.

Rodney was preparing to make a long jump shot when he heard Tyray's voice. Hesitating for a second, he shot the ball, missing the basket completely.

"Air ball," the other boy joked, getting the rebound.

Rodney scowled at the boy and then slowly walked over to Tyray.

"What's up?" Rodney asked.

"You turned on me, Banks. The minute the cash stopped rolling in, you were history," Tyray said bitterly. Rodney looked at Tyray, watching him carefully but saying nothing.

"I've got me a gun, Banks," Tyray continued, opening his coat so Rodney could see the weapon.

"Say what?" Rodney gasped, looking into his pocket. "Boy, are you crazy?"

"Shut up, Banks," Tyray said sharply. "You were one of the ones who turned on me, and you know it, so don't start givin' me static. Now listen up. I'm settlin' a lot of scores, and if you don't wanna be one of them, you're gonna do me a favor. You tell everyone that the time for dissin' Tyray Hobbs is over. You put the fear into them, Banks. I want things back like old times."

"What are you gonna do?" Rodney asked, beads of sweat forming on his forehead.

Looking at the fear in Rodney's face, Tyray felt powerful. It was as if he had grown taller since he had gotten the gun. "Don't you worry about it, Banks. You just do what I say, and you and me won't have no problems."

"Yeah, sure," Rodney said, his eyes wide with worry. "Whatever you say."

"I want Darrell Mercer to sweat. You let him know what's comin' down. You make sure he knows I'm comin' for him," Tyray said.

"I'll do it."

"He may have hit me with a cheap shot in the cafeteria, but I ain't done with him yet. He's gonna wish he never met me." As he spoke, Tyray stepped closer to Rodney, and in one swift motion, he pulled out the gun and shoved it into Rodney's stomach.

"Tyray, no!" he pleaded, recoiling in fear.

Tyray withdrew the gun and smiled. "That's more like it," he said with a smirk. Tyray felt better than he had in days. The gun felt comfortable in his hand, as if he had owned it forever. He looked forward to the coming week.

He could not wait to see Darrell's face when he emerged from a shadow, pointing his gun at the boy's chest.

Chapter 10

On Monday morning, Tyray sensed that word about the gun was spreading through Bluford.

By lunchtime, freshmen were treating him differently. Jamee Wills, who usually scoffed at him, looked down and darted off in another direction when he approached her in the hallway. Others who had snickered when Tyray walked by now steered clear of him. For the first time in days, Tyray walked through the halls with his shoulders thrown back and his head high.

In the cafeteria, Tyray spotted Darrell. Almost mechanically, he found himself approaching Darrell's table. As he got closer, he noticed Harold was watching him, his face stricken as if he saw a ghost.

"Hi, there, Mercer," Tyray said, looking directly at Darrell. A hush seemed to fall over the cafeteria.

"Hi," Darrell answered, his eyes shifting to Tyray's hands.

He's looking for the gun, Tyray thought.

"I see you eatin' the cafeteria food," Tyray said. "S'posed to be bad for your health." Darrell did not say anything, but Tyray saw something familiar in the boy's eyes—fear. "But I guess it'll take a long time for that stuff to kill you," Tyray added before walking away.

After lunch, Tyray was called to the principal's office. He had hoped word of the gun would not reach any Bluford teachers. As he entered Ms. Spencer's office, he felt nervous. She had a stern look on her face. "Well, Mr. Hobbs," she said coldly. "Have we got a problem?"

Tyray smiled politely. "No, ma'am. Not me. Everything's cool. I'm studyin' and keepin' outta trouble."

Ms. Spencer eyed him warily. He knew she was no fool. "I've heard rumors that you're starting to intimidate kids again. There's even talk that you have a gun. I don't know if any of this is true, so I thought I'd ask you. Is any of this true? If it is, tell me now, and let me help you. I don't want to see you ruin your life or harm anyone else."

"Hey, I ain't got no gun, Ms. Spencer. I know we got this zero-tolerance rule about weapons, and that's a good thing. I got to tell you though, Ms. Spencer, Darrell Mercer likes to spread lies about me. Most likely he's the one spreadin' those rumors."

"Then you would have no objections to a check of your backpack and locker?" Ms. Spencer asked.

"That's just fine. I got nothin' to hide," Tyray said, beginning to empty his backpack on the principal's desk. He knew better than to bring his gun to school. After Ms. Spencer thoroughly inspected each pocket of his backpack, she escorted him to his locker. Two hallway monitors accompanied them.

"I told you I ain't got a gun," he said as they examined his locker. Ms. Spencer watched in grim silence.

After the locker was checked, Tyray returned to his classes. Students' heads turned nervously as he walked to his desk.

"Whatcha lookin' at?" he asked, knowing no one would dare answer him.

By the end of the day, Tyray could see the nervous tension in the eyes of many students passing him in the hallway.

Even Shamar and Cedric eyed him nervously as he walked out of the building.

Outside, he felt a hand grab his arm. He turned to find Lark standing next to him.

"Tyray, what's happening around here?" she asked. "Everyone says you're after Darrell Mercer and you got a gun. Is that true?"

"Who said that?" Tyray said, pretending to be shocked.

Lark put her hand on Tyray's shoulder and stared into his eyes. "Tyray, I care about you, honest I do, but if you did something stupid like getting a gun and—"

"Look, I don't wanna talk about it no more," Tyray said, avoiding her gaze.

"Tyray, Darrell didn't mean anything against you. He was just scared of you is all. Can't you just forget all the stuff that happened?" Lark said.

Tyray glared at Lark. "Oh, so now you sidin' with him too? Girl, just leave me alone."

"I wish you'd change," Lark pleaded. "Tyray, I've liked you from the beginning because I thought I saw something in you that nobody else could see. I thought you were different from what everybody else said. I thought that no one ever gave you a chance."

"Yeah, well maybe you thought wrong," Tyray growled. "I'm what everyone says. I'm bad, and you should just stay away from me." He had to get away from Lark. Something about her was getting to him, was twisting him inside. No matter how hard he fought it, it was there. "I gotta go," he muttered, turning to walk away.

"Tyray, listen to me! Stop whatever it is you're planning. This thing with Darrell should have ended a long time ago. It's got to stop. Just go talk to him. He's working at the grocery store until 8:00 tonight. Why don't you call him after he gets home?"

Tyray turned back and looked at Lark. For a second, he considered her idea, but just as quickly, he dismissed it. If he called, Darrell would win, and Tyray would be the loser once again. He could not let that happen.

"I ain't callin' no one," he said, walking towards home.

"But Tyray . . . ," Lark began. Her voice grated on his nerves. He ignored her and kept walking.

Tyray got home before his parents and found a message on the answering machine. It was from his mother, asking him to call her at work as soon as he got home. Tyray knew from the sound of her voice that she was worried. Maybe Ms. Spencer called her. If so, it was only a matter of time before Dad found out what was happening.

Tyray felt as if the world was closing in on him. Chills ran through Tyray's body, and his thoughts began spinning wildly. He dreaded the hour his father returned, and he knew not to call his mother. She would panic, and then he would have to deal with both of his parents. Tyray felt like an animal backed into a corner. Darrell was going to win again.

Tyray raced to his room and grabbed the gun. He had to be gone before his parents made it home. Hiding the gun under his belt, he bolted from the house. It was 4:00, and gray clouds were gathering overhead. Tyray knew he had to act tonight. If his parents found out about the gun, he would be in the worst trouble of his life. He knew his father would beat him, maybe even disown him as he had Warren. Ms. Spencer would certainly kick him out of school. There would be nothing left for him but the torment of other kids, or worse—jail.

If I'm goin' down, thought Tyray as he reached a park, *Mercer is goin' down with me.*

At 6:00, a fine drizzle began to fall. Tyray escaped it by going into a local arcade. It was a place he and Warren would sometimes go when they needed to get away from Dad.

Tyray watched as kids took turns shooting villains on a large video screen. The bodies flashed for a second when they were hit and then disappeared. Tyray remembered how he and his brother used to play such games. He pushed the memory from his mind, fighting back tears. He missed Warren desperately, but he was alone now, and nothing would change that.

Tyray kept an eye on the arcade's windows, watching as darkness descended on the neighborhood. He felt a knot in the pit of his stomach as he imagined the events to come.

Heading out into the steady drizzle, Tyray walked towards the store where Darrell worked. Making sure not to draw attention to himself, he scoped out the spot where he thought he had the best chance of surprising Darrell. It was an alley lined by thick bushes behind some boarded-up garages.

On other days, Tyray had seen Darrell bike through the alley on his way to work. He knew that with the thick misty darkness, he could hide undetected in the shadows until Darrell appeared. He would just wait for him and then jump out, knock Darrell off his bike, and do it. It was as simple as that.

BANG-BANG, it would all be over, just like the video game. All he had to do was wait.

Tyray took his position in a group of bushes between two garages. It was 7:45. A scrawny kitten appeared at his feet. Its eyes glowed an odd green in the dark night. "Go away," Tyray whispered harshly, pushing the animal away with his foot.

Tyray's heart was pounding as he waited. He felt his blood rushing through his veins. Tyray wondered if Bones had felt the same way. Tyray grabbed the gun, feeling its weight in his hand, the metal still warm from the heat of his stomach.

Suddenly, Tyray heard the clank and rattle of a bicycle approaching. Tyray's right hand tightened on the revolver. His left hand, still in a cast, tingled with anticipation. A second later, the bike appeared.

It turned down the alley as Tyray expected. Darrell Mercer pedaled, quickly veering around puddles to get home. He looked smaller than Tyray remembered. Riding the bike, he appeared to be much younger than a high school student. Tyray's muscles tensed as he prepared to attack.

He waited until an instant before the bike passed him. Exploding from the darkness, Tyray lunged at Darrell, side-swiping him with his shoulder. The impact caught Darrell by surprise, sending him crashing into the garage wall, the bike tumbling just ahead of him. Darrell grunted as his body came to a rest in a shallow puddle.

Tyray walked over to him, aiming the gun at his face.

"I got you, man," Tyray said.

Darrell looked up, his eyes wide open in terror. "Man, please don't kill me," he begged, putting his hand over his head to protect himself. Tyray could see his jaw trembling as he spoke.

Cowering on the ground, Darrell seemed smaller than ever. And he was helpless. For an instant, he reminded Tyray of the small puppy from years earlier. Shaking off the memory, Tyray hesitated.

The alley was quiet except for the gentle drip of the light rain that was falling.

"I thought you were different from what everybody else said," Lark's words echoed through his mind.

But Lark was wrong, Tyray thought. This was his chance to get back respect, to show everyone who was boss, to be a man. Tyray's finger moved to the trigger.

"Please don't kill me," Darrell repeated, tears running down his face.

"I remember him when he was dying . . . the way his eyes went wild and his cheeks puffed out . . . the blood and all." Now, Bones's words came back to him.

"Be the last face you see every night . . . the last face you see before you die."

The gun trembled in Tyray's wet hand.

"I always knew you were headed for trouble."

Tyray's thoughts raced ahead with images of the future. He saw Darrell lying on the ground in a pool of blood. He saw Lark looking at him in disgust. He saw his mother crying. He saw Warren's saddened face, his father's unforgiving scowl. And he saw himself able to make it all different, right now.

Tyray looked closely at Darrell. The boy's face was scratched from the fall, and in the rain, he looked to be about twelve years old. Just one flick of the finger, and he would be gone. Just like the boy Bones killed, like the puppy Dad kicked out. Tyray could be just like both men—and he would be a monster.

But if he did not shoot Darrell, he would fail again. And he would be in trouble, the worst of his life. His father would beat him. Ms. Spencer would expel him. Kids would think he was a psycho, a loser. It was too late to avoid that now. Even if Darrell did walk away, Tyray knew his own life was ruined. *"It's too late for me,"* he thought.

"Whatever you do, don't end up like me," Warren's voice whispered in Tyray's mind.

Tyray raised the gun away from Darrell's face. Tears now mixed with rain on Tyray's cheek. He turned the gun towards himself, placing it against the side of his face, his vision clouded with tears.

"Tyray, don't!" Darrell said, springing quickly from the ground.

BANG!

Tyray felt the heat of the gunshot, heard the deafening pop, saw the blinding flash and smelled the fiery gunpowder. Then he felt himself falling, almost in slow motion.

But an instant before that, he felt an impact against his chest and sensed his arm being wrenched away from his body. Darrell had charged him, and the two boys tumbled to the ground together. The gun was between them, aiming upwards and away. The shot had gone into the air. Both boys' hands were on the weapon when they hit the muddy cement.

"Let go!" Darrell screamed, struggling to pry the weapon from Tyray's hand.

Tyray relaxed his fingers, and Darrell yanked the gun away, throwing it into the thick darkness of the alley.

"Man, you shoulda let me do it," Tyray cried, tears pouring from his eyes. He sat up in the puddle and shook his head. Darrell stood up next to him. "I ain't got nothin' else, man. You took it all away. Besides, my dad's gonna kill me anyway."

Darrell turned, grabbed his bike, and started to walk away, but then he stopped and looked back at Tyray.

"So now you lookin' down on me too. You just wanna pity me, right?" Tyray said bitterly, struggling unsuccessfully to stop crying.

Darrell stood motionless for several seconds. "Come on," he said finally in a shaky voice, walking back over to Tyray and offering his hand. A scrape ran along Darrell's forehead from when he fell off his bike, but his hand was outstretched. The gesture made Tyray feel even sadder, and for once he made no effort to hide it.

"Man, I need help," Tyray said, shaking his head. "I'm in so much trouble. It ain't never been like this."

"Come on," Darrell urged. "It don't have to be this way."

Tyray closed his eyes. He wanted the words to be true. He was tired of fighting, of keeping everything inside, of lying, of being Tyray Hobbs, the bully that made other kids run. That path left him alone and friendless. It left him in dark alleys with a gun. It nearly made him a killer. But Tyray did not know where to begin, or how to change, or what to do.

Reaching up, Tyray grasped Darrell's wet and muddy hand, and the boy pulled him up.

In the distance, a police siren echoed through the dark corridors of the city.

"I won't tell anyone about this,"

Darrell said. "No one has to know but me and you."

Tyray looked at the boy. For once, he knew that he had avoided a mistake, and he was grateful that Darrell stood before him. Darrell was proof Tyray was not Bones. He was not a monster, a killer of kids. He was something else, something that was not totally bad. Maybe even something that could be good.

"Darrell, I'm sorry, man," he said.

"Hey, I'm just glad we're both standin'," Darrell said with a hint of a smile.

"Me too, man," Tyray said, his eyes misty again. "Me too."

Together, the two boys walked in silence down the dark alley. At its end, they headed in opposite directions. Tyray wasn't sure if they would ever be friends, but he knew as they parted they were no longer enemies.

When he approached his front steps, Tyray was afraid to go in, scared of what would happen in the hours, days, and weeks ahead. He dreaded facing his parents, especially his father. But the road ahead was not as bad as the path behind him, one of guns, criminals, and dark alleys.

Tyray wiped his eyes, took a deep breath, and stepped inside.

The first person Tyray saw was Mr. Mitchell, sitting in the living room speaking to his father. Both men stopped talking as soon as he opened the door.

"Tyray!" his mother exclaimed, rushing over and hugging him. "Where have you been?"

"You okay?" his father asked, looking at him with concern. Tyray glanced at his parents in confusion.

"I'm fine. What's going on?" Tyray asked, taking a step back and glancing at Mr. Mitchell.

"I came over here to talk to your parents," Mr. Mitchell said. "We've been worried about you."

"He called this afternoon," his mother explained, "and when I got home, I found a bloody pillowcase and this in your room." She pulled a crumpled piece of paper from her pocket. Tyray knew it was the letter to Warren he had started to write and tossed into the trash can. "We were so worried, we called Mr. Mitchell, and he came right over."

"Mr. Mitchell's a good man. He's been talkin' some sense to me," Dad explained, his eyes puffy and red. "I already lost one son. I ain't gonna lose another one. What happened tonight, Tyray? What kinda trouble did you get yourself into?"

Tyray swallowed hard. He knew he had to tell them the truth. Part of him looked forward to it. For once, he would say what was on his mind, what had pushed him to the edge. He would admit what happened with Darrell, his feelings of desperation, his anger at his father, and his quest for the gun. And he would tell them about Warren, about how he would like to visit him, and how his letter had helped Tyray avoid an act that would have ruined his life.

"Nothin' bad happened. You didn't lose nobody, Dad. Not me or Warren. You never did." Tyray said. He felt strangely calm and relieved. For once, both his parents were listening, a teacher was on his side, and he hadn't hurt anyone.

A tear rolled down Tyray's cheek as he looked at the three people watching him. Outside, a police siren wailed, momentarily moving closer and then passing by, racing to some other part of the city. Racing away from Tyray's home.

Tyray took a deep breath and began to tell his story.

Until We Meet Again

The summer was supposed to be different.

With the school year over, Darcy Wills looked forward to the best time of her life. But her plans are shattered by a series of unexpected events. First, horrible news threatens to rip her boyfriend Hakeem away. And then someone new enters her life, leaving Darcy in a world of confusion. Before the summer ends, Darcy makes choices that profoundly change her, and a beloved piece of her world is lost forever.

Turn the page for a special sneak preview. . . .

"Girls, sit down. Your father and I have something important to tell you."

Darcy Wills glanced at her sister Jamee, wondering if she knew what their mother was about to announce. Jamee, fourteen years old and two years younger than Darcy, shrugged her shoulders and sat down at the table.

"We've been doing a lot of thinking lately," Mom said nervously, sitting down at the head of the table. Darcy's father sat beside her, gently holding her hand. "We've decided to give our marriage a second chance."

Darcy's heart jumped into her throat, and Jamee nearly fell out of her chair.

"For real!" Jamee cheered, putting her hands on either side of her face as if she could barely believe what she just heard.

"That's right," her father added. "We've been going to counseling and we're gonna try and make it work, for us, for you two, and for Grandma." Dad's eyes glistened as he spoke, and Darcy knew he meant every word.

Only months ago, he had reappeared after a five-year absence. Darcy was just eleven years old when he abandoned the family. For years, she had made up stories to explain why he had left. But later, when she found out that he had taken off with another woman, Darcy decided she would never forgive him for the hurt he caused.

Then, last fall, he came back like a stranger one evening. Since that time, he did everything he could to help Darcy, Jamee, and their mother. He even admitted his mistakes, apologized to each of them, and swore to be a father again. At first, Darcy did not believe him, but months had passed, and he was still there, offering advice, support, and love. And now this.

"Girls, I understand this might be difficult. I'm not going to forget what your father did, and I don't expect you to either," Mom added, looking at her husband. "But he's a different man now. I believe what he says, and we both want us to be a family again."

Before Mom finished her sentence, Jamee got up and hugged her parents. "I'm so happy," she repeated over and over again.

Darcy quickly followed, putting her arms around her parents. The years of bitterness seemed to thaw in the embrace. Even though part of her was still angry at her father, another bigger part was thrilled that he was back and that he wanted to be with them.

"There's something else we want to tell you," Mom said, gently pulling away from the hug. "We're moving."

"What?" Darcy yelled, pretending to be surprised. Her father had admitted to Jamee and Darcy that he wanted to move the family out of their old apartment and into a nearby house. He had even taken Darcy and her sister to see the house, though he never promised them he would buy it.

"We found a small house a few blocks away. It's so close you two will still able to go to Bluford High School, but it has more room and a nice little yard for Grandma," Mom explained. "We'll be moving in about a week."

"I can't believe this. Wait till I tell everyone at school!" Jamee said with a wide toothy smile. Darcy agreed. She couldn't wait to tell her friends about the sudden changes in her life.

As she got ready for bed that night, Darcy wondered if there were any other surprises in store for her in the days ahead.

The next morning, Darcy raced off to Bluford High, eager to tell her boyfriend Hakeem the good news about her family. Over the past year, Darcy and Hakeem had become very close. Months ago, he helped her deal with the sudden arrival of her father and was supportive weeks later when Jamee ran away from home. Darcy got even closer to Hakeem when he told her his father had been diagnosed with cancer earlier in the year. At least now, Darcy figured, she had something good to share with him. As she reached school, Darcy spotted Hakeem riding his silver motorbike into the school parking lot.

"Hakeem!" she cried, running over to him. "I've got the best news! My parents are getting back together, and we're moving into a new house with a back-yard and everything!"

Hakeem gave Darcy a hug, but she felt right away that there was something wrong. His arms were like dead weights around her, and the embrace did not last long before Hakeem pulled away.

"That's great, Darcy," he said, getting off the motorbike. He began to walk ahead, shoulders down and staring at the ground. Darcy remained a few steps behind, stunned.

"Hakeem, is everything okay?"

Hakeem stopped and slowly turned to look at her. "D-dad c-can't handle the job like he used to," said Hakeem, stuttering as he often did when nervous, "not since the chemotherapy t-treatments. That cancer really whipped him bad. He works two or three hours, then he's no good for the rest of the day."

Darcy walked up to Hakeem and took his hand. "I'm sorry, Hakeem," she said, suddenly feeling foolish.

"It's not good," Hakeem continued, shaking his head. "Dad's brother has a store in Detroit, where they sell furniture and TV's and stuff, and he's offered Dad a job there. It would be a lot easier for him to handle, mostly keeping up with the inventory. Dad's real good with numbers. He just can't work real long hours, that's all."

Darcy felt as if her heart had dropped into her knees. *Detroit?* It was so far from California, it might as well be another planet. For a second, Darcy's tongue felt glued to the back of her throat, and she was unable to speak.

"So does this mean you're going to move?" she asked.

"Yeah, if Dad takes the job," Hakeem said somberly. "He hasn't made up his mind yet. He said he needs to talk to his doctors. But if he decides to take it, we would leave as soon as the school year ends."

Darcy's mind spun like a whirlwind. Waking up this morning, Darcy felt as if her life was on a wonderful upswing, and nothing could go wrong. Now everything felt different. Just as quickly as she had gotten her family back, Darcy was now at risk of losing her boyfriend.

"I . . . I don't know what to say," Darcy stammered, forcing back tears.

"Nothing is definite yet," Hakeem assured her. "I just wanted you to know that I might have to move away."

Hakeem's last words seemed to hang in the air. *Move away.* Just minutes earlier she had so many plans for the summer. Now all that was threatened.

"You can't leave Bluford now," she declared. "I mean, don't you have a relative or someone you could live with? Maybe you could stay with Cooper or something." Cooper Hodden was one of Hakeem and Darcy's closest friends. She was sure Cooper would let Hakeem stay with his family. Even as she spoke, Darcy knew she was being selfish, but she could not stop herself. She felt as if someone was robbing her.

"I can't leave my family, Darcy. They depend on me," Hakeem said, stepping away from her, as if something she said pained him. "Look, I don't know how this is all gonna turn out. The doctors don't even know, not yet. But if Mom and Dad and the rest of the kids have to go to Detroit, then I have to be there, too. I don't want to go, but—"

The school bell rang loudly, signaling the start of morning classes. "We gotta go, Darcy. We'll talk about this later." Hakeem quickly turned and rushed into the building, leaving Darcy alone in the parking lot.

Tarah Carson, Darcy's closest friend, shook her head when Darcy told her Hakeem might be moving. They were standing at a water fountain between classes. "Girl," Tarah said, "Hakeem's father is real sick. That chemo is tough to handle. I know because my neighbor went through it, and he ain't been himself ever since."

"But what about *us*?" Darcy wailed. "This was supposed to be our first summer together."

"Listen, Darcy. Right now Hakeem's gotta do what he can for his family. They're all goin' through this, not just him. His little sisters and his mother are sufferin' too," Tarah explained.

"I know what you're saying, and I feel bad for them, especially for his dad," Darcy said, wiping her eyes. "But at the same time, I feel so bad for me, too. Is that wrong, Tarah? Am I a bad person to feel that way?"

"No, Hakeem's your boyfriend. Of course you don't want to see him go! If someone told me Cooper had to move, I don't know what I'd do," she admitted, giving Darcy a sympathetic hug. "But you gotta put yourself in his shoes too."

Darcy nodded. "Thanks, Tarah," she said, fighting back more tears. She knew Tarah was right. Moving would be harder on Hakeem than anyone else. Besides worrying about his father, he would be losing everything—his school, his friends, his neighborhood, and her. But understanding Hakeem's troubles only made her feel worse. *What about us?* she thought to herself again, dread gathering in her chest like storm clouds in a summer sky.

After school, Darcy went straight home. She wasn't in the mood to talk to anyone. Normally, she would go into her bedroom when she wanted to be alone, but now her room was cluttered with boxes in preparation for moving into the new house. Frustrated, she sat in the living room and flipped through a magazine. Jamee arrived from school a few minutes later.

"Hey, Darcy, guess what?" Jamee said, throwing her school bag on the couch. "Liselle Mason, the girl who lives across the street, wants to hire you."

"Hire me? For what?" Darcy asked. "I hardly know her." Liselle had been a junior at Bluford when Darcy was in eighth grade. All Darcy remembered about Liselle was that she had been popular until she got pregnant and dropped out of Bluford. Once in a while, Darcy saw Liselle at the grocery store, but she never said more than a quick hello.

"I ran into her outside, and she told me she needs a babysitter. She asked me if you were available," Jamee said, fishing a piece of paper from her pocket. "She needs someone to watch her baby while she goes back to school. Here's her phone number. I told her you'd call her."

Darcy was surprised by Liselle's offer. Still, she could use the money. And working would be better than sitting around feeling sorry for herself if Hakeem left, she thought. "Thanks. I'll call her tonight," Darcy said, getting up from the couch to check on Grandma.

In the darkened bedroom, Darcy found Grandma sitting in her chair staring into space.

"Hey, Grandma," Darcy said, kneeling down and taking her grandmother's thickly-veined hand. "We're gonna move into our new house soon. That'll be so good. We're gonna have a backyard and you can watch the birds—"

"I'm cold," Grandma declared, even though it was warm in the apartment. "Why isn't the heater on?"

"I'll get your shawl, Grandma," Darcy said. She went to the nearby dresser and reached into the top drawer.

"Is that better?" she asked, draping the shawl on Grandma's thin shoulders.

"No," she snapped. "It's still cold."

Darcy noticed that her grandmother seemed to be having more cranky spells lately. *Could her condition be worsening?* Darcy wondered. Ever since Grandma's first stroke over a year ago, Darcy feared that the family might be forced to send Grandma to a nursing home. She imagined her grandmother calling out her name in the middle of the night, only to have a stranger appear at her bedside. The thought of Grandma alone and frightened in unfamiliar surroundings made Darcy shudder. There was no way she would allow Grandma to be put into such a place. No way.

After dinner, Darcy called Liselle Mason. "Thanks for calling," Liselle said. "I guess your sister told you why I asked you to call."

"Yes," Darcy replied. "She said you were looking for a babysitter."

"That's right. I'm heading back to school this summer, and I wanted to know if you'd be interested in babysitting my daughter a couple days a week. She's just two years old, but she's an angel."

"I'd love to watch her for you," Darcy said, trying to sound enthusiastic, though her thoughts kept drifting back to Hakeem. Darcy agreed to visit Liselle's apartment and meet the baby after school the next day. As soon as she hung up the phone with Liselle, Darcy tried to call Hakeem, but his phone was busy. She gave up after two more attempts.

Why doesn't he call me? she wondered as she lay in bed that night. Her small bedroom was almost completely packed and ready to be moved. In the darkness, the shadows of boxes and the stale smell of cardboard made her room seem eerie and unfamiliar. Everything she had grown used to seemed to be changing. Some of it was good, and some was bad. But it was all different, and Darcy felt powerless to stop it.

"I wish some things never changed," Darcy whispered, thinking of Hakeem and wondering why he didn't call.

Read all about your favorite characters from Bluford High!

A mysterious stranger is following Darcy Wills and she's getting threatening notes at school. When her sister suddenly disappears, Darcy finds herself in a race against time.

Darcy Wills and Brisana Meeks used to be friends, but all that changed when Darcy started hanging with "the zeros." Now Brisana is after Darcy's boyfriend, and Darcy must face her old friend again.